T0062353

About the Book

Pearce's infidelity. Park Lane's treasure. Angela's future.

Angela and Pearce were like any other happy young African American couple in Los Angeles in the early 1970s. But that all came crashing to an end when Pearce told his pregnant wife, Angela, the police were after him for a robbery he didn't commit. The young girl's heart said, "Whither thou goest...." and she left her home and family to flee with the husband she loved to Valdosta, Georgia. She settled into an isolated existence in a little community on Park Lane.

Angela kept to herself until one morning when, nine months pregnant, she discovered Pearce was seeing another woman. Through the pain of Pearce's lies came her own awakening. Angela grew into herself, recognizing things she had denied for so long, and took dominion over her future. This is her story.

A Fugitive's Wife

A Fugitive's

A Tale of Humanity, Infidelity
and the Triumph
of the Human Spirit

Abrendal Austin

Riverside, California

A Fugitive's Wife

Copyright © 2005 Abrendal Austin

Published by Black Penny Press
5198 Arlington Ave. #923
Riverside, CA 92504
877-741-7651 • FAX 951-848-9355
info@blackpennypress.com • www.blackpennypress.com
951 - 741 - 7651

Publisher's Cataloguing-in-Publication

Austin, Abrendal.
    A fugitive's wife : a tale of humanity, infidelity and the triumph of the human spirit / Abrendal Austin. -- 1st ed. -- Riverside, CA : Black Penny Press, 2005.

    p. ; cm.

    ISBN: 0-9748066-7-6

    1. Fugitives from justice--Fiction. 2. Man-woman relationships--Fiction. 3. Interpersonal relations--Fiction. 4. Self-reliance--Fiction. 5. Bildungsromans. I. Title.

PS3601.U885 F84 2005   2004095827
813.6--dc22   0501

Printed and bound in the United States of America - Acid-Free Paper

Book Consultant: Ellen Reid
Cover Design: Dotti Albertine
Book Design: Patricia Bacall
Author Photos: Bob Hankins

I dedicate this book to my wonderful, beautiful, hard-working family and friends for all the love and support given to me and to each other.

Never give up on your dreams.

Acknowledgements

Thanks a million times to the following people for their superior talents: Laren Bright, copywriter; Dotti Albertine, cover designer; Patricia Bacall, graphic designer and production coordinator; Brookes Nohlgren, editor; and the world's best Diva book shepherd, Ellen Reid.

Prologue

*I*n Valdosta, Georgia, folks set outside day and night. It didn't matter if it was ninety degrees and the humidity reached eighty percent. Inside their shabby duplexes, there were probably less flies to swat. Children ran around barefoot wearing what skimpy clothes they could get by with. Short pants showed off mosquito bites on their dusty legs, and flies buzzed around their sticky hands and brown faces. They still enjoyed playing hide and seek, climbing pecan trees, making mud pies and chasing squawking chickens around the yard.

Grown folks sat on stoops, milk crates and old wooden porches. In between fanning annoying flies and slapping mosquitoes, they sipped ice-cold Coca Colas, puffed cigarettes and gave little children extra change to run back and forth to the corner store. They lived outside almost as much as they did inside. Women forced their girls to sit still while they put tight braids into their hair to last until next week's shampoo.

When Miss Dixie Mae hollered down the lane and asked Miss Susie if she was going to Bible Study, she didn't care that the whole neighborhood heard her. It was just too hot to walk six houses down the lane. So everybody knew if they were going to church.

The most exciting thing that happened lately was Old Buster caught thirty-five catfish at Nash's fishing hole. He sat on an old milk crate cleaning his catch in a banged-up washtub. The portable fan set up in the yard did little to cool the sweat dripping down his fat, naked belly.

His wife, Dixie Mae, fried the cats up quick on that hot night. Folks came and brought huge, sweet watermelons, ice-cold beer, soda pop and banana pudding. After all the eating was over, the kids played hide and seek, fought over marbles and threw water balloons. The mamas and daddies sipped beer, played dominoes and pity-pat and sang along with Aretha Franklin and B.B. King on the stereo.

The old folks sat around in rocking chairs, chewing tobacco, eating boiled peanuts and seeing who could tell the biggest tales.

The teenagers discussed ways to get to college, the latest and greatest pop and soul singers and who would be the first on the lane to get rich.

Life was like that in Valdosta, Georgia, in the 1970s. It's probably pretty much the same today.

Chapter 1

*A*ngela Jones sucked in her breath hard when her fingers pulled a red package of rubbers from her husband's, Pearce's, shirt pocket. Rage rippled through her aching, swollen body like a savage roller coaster. She stopped cleaning the one-bedroom duplex. In a state of shock with sweat dripping from her armpits, she eased her body onto the lumpy mattress and tossed the white shirt over the side chair as though it were on fire.

Her unborn child kicked and assaulted her insides, forcing her to grab her huge belly and cry out, "Oh, God, please give me strength to go on."

Angela believed very much that God wanted her to be with her husband even if he was wanted by the F.B.I. Pearce didn't want to go to jail for a robbery that he said he was framed for. He said a black man never did and never would have a fair chance to prove his innocence. When he asked her to run with him from Los Angeles, California, to Valdosta, Georgia, she heard a voice saying, "Wither thou goest, I will follow." Now after seeing the rubbers in his shirt pocket, she figured the God she served had been wrong.

Trembling, hot and sweaty, she shuffled her big body into the tiny kitchen, punched the button on the portable fan and allowed the soft breeze to wave her flowered dress, cooling her hot, brown skin.

The Sunday morning sunlight filtered through the dingy blue café curtains, crinkling the faded blue wallpaper above the old, potbellied stove. The musty smell of rotten wood seeped through the ragged, tiled floor. A long, shallow sink was worn and rusted by the constant drip of the single faucet. A cast-iron pot sat underneath to catch the water missed by the poorly taped elbow pipe. A mixture of full-grown cockroaches and red ants had found their final resting place in it during the night. Angela forced the window up and breathed in the warm fragrance of the jasmine, pink roses and white carnations she had planted in the small backyard. A pair of black-and-white, orange-striped butterflies fluttered from one bloom to another.

The flowerbed, one of the few pleasant sights, lined the far side of a walkway of uneven red bricks. The other side, which bordered the duplex, was cluttered with anthills and clay sand.

The sound of dripping water took her to the pot under the sink. She gathered the courage to empty it and thought back to a time in her junior high school when the class was listening attentively to a poem called "Evangeline." Suddenly Tommy Mason, who sat next to her, cried out, "It's a roach, crawling on the floor."

Somehow Angela was sure it had come from her overstuffed purse sitting on the floor.

She bent over now, picked up the pot and tossed the contents into the flowerbed, just missing an eight-inch lizard running across the rickety picket fence. She lit the burner of the stove and began to press her black afro hairdo into a straight style. Her stiff fingers trembled when she placed the iron comb on the yellow and blue flame.

She set the makeup mirror on the dining table, sat in a chair and fiercely combed her kinky hair as if to wake herself from a nightmare.

Dancing footsteps echoing on the squeaky tiled floor startled Angela. Pearce had arrived. Her heart began to pound. She felt every jagged nerve from her head to her swollen toes.

Pearce's dark chocolate face had a long, wide nose you could see right into. Wavy brown hair lay on his broad shoulders. A matching mustache curled at the ends, moved up and down whenever he frowned or flashed an infectious smile. White cut-off jeans showed off his lean, muscular legs.

Angela continued styling her hair as he approached her and quickly studied his smiling face for signs of guilt.

"Happy Birthday, baby. I know you thought I forgot. How does it feel being twenty-one?" He leaned down to kiss her lips but she turned away and caught his mouth on her cheek. Pearce straightened up and silently walked to the sink to wash his hands.

Angela stood up, took the hot comb in her right hand, took three slow steps towards him and stopped. She then walked right past him. "It's hot in here," she said and slammed the back door against the wall. Without saying another word, she set the comb on the stove, turned it off and cleared her things off the table.

Pearce dried his hands, "I'm gonna buy you that dress you saw the other day for your birthday, and how come you been pressing your hair? You know I don't like that straight shit."

Angela stared him straight into those honey eyes, her hands on her hips, "And just why don't you tell me what the hell kinda hair you do like. And while you're at it, tell me who you were with last night? Don't lie because I found your rubbers in your shirt pocket this morning!"

Pearce walked into the bedroom, Angela right behind him, and picked up the shirt. "Aw, baby, I found these on the floor at the pool hall last night. You know you are the only woman in my life."

"I really don't believe that now, and I always trusted you. Even when you said you were not involved in that robbery. I put all my faith in you. I'm pretty sure I hate your guts right now. This is hurting me too much. Too much, Pearce. Where did you go this morning?"

"I had to go buy a new battery for the car." He laid back on the bed with his hands under his head.

"Where's the receipt? Show it to me."

"I left it in the car. Gimme a break. Damn!" He turned over, put the pillow on top of his head and closed his eyes. Angela walked to the front of the living room and pushed open the torn screen door. "I'll go and get it," she called back to him.

Pearce raced past her out the door and down the narrow walkway to his 1956 green Chevy. Angela, determined to find out the truth, hurried to the car only to find him looking in the glove compartment. She walked to the driver's side of the car, opened the door and sat on the cool, vinyl seat. What looked like a greeting card stuck out from behind the left sun visor. He did not see her take it and open it. When she opened it, she saw a picture of Pearce and Danielle Spencer, the redheaded bitch who lived down the street, who Angela did ironing for. They were hugging and smiling.

The inscription said, "Having a good time at the Satin Slipper, June 2, 1972."

Angela got out of the car slowly, and quickly walked down Park Lane.

Pearce hurried beside her, desperation on his face, "Come back, baby. Danielle's not even home now. It's just a silly picture."

Suddenly Angela felt her stomach wrench with knife pains, but she kept on marching down Park Lane in the ninety-degree heat and humidity. She felt like a soldier going to war, swinging the folder in her right hand. "Just don't touch me. I'm going to see this bitch right now. I'm going to get the truth 'cause you think I'm crazy. And you know what? I am going to kill this bitch right now!"

Pearce grabbed her arm, "Wait. I'll tell you the truth. Just come back to the house. Come back inside." Angela stopped, almost out of breath, turned around and walked towards the house. He stood watching her. She felt knife pains again. She sucked in her breath and her voice weakened. "I don't want anything anymore but the truth."

She ripped the picture in half, threw it into a beat-up trashcan and walked slowly to the front door. She opened the screen, glanced back and saw Pearce reach down and take the picture out of the trash. A big, silly grin on his face.

Angela turned around, slammed the door and went right back down Park Lane towards Danielle's house.

Chapter 2

Buster laid his fish scaler on the table and yelled, "Dixie Mae, where you think that pregnant Miss Angela going like she racing for something? That red dress just a waving and them big pretty legs is moving!"

The sweet fragrance of Dixie Mae's coconut shampoo floated thru the warm air to Buster's nose, giving him a pleasant break from the fish smell. She came to the screen door with a towel wrapped around her silver and black hair and suds dripping down her tawny face. Her pencil-thin eyebrows wrinkled, and her dark eyes silenced him. "Oh hush, you old fool. I guess she's going to see that wild child Danielle. You and everybody know Pearce is messing around with her."

"Yeah you right, Dixie Mae, but I know Miss Angela ain't over twenty yet. That gal stay in the house all the time. Seems like she don't go nowhere but in that yard fooling with those flowers. And I know he works."

Dixie Mae toweled her hair. "Buster, it's like she scared to come out and get to know people. You know I tried to get her to come to the fish fry the other night. She gave me those red roses for decorating but she never showed up. I knew something was going to happen. I hear she waits on him hand and foot. That's the problem. She's too nice to that fool."

Buster rinsed his hands with the cool water from the hose and dried them on his old cloth. "Well, Dixie Mae, she ain't thinking nothing too nice this morning." He decided to take action and planted himself directly in Angela's path with his long, sun-blackened arms folded over his fat, naked belly. He stood six feet tall with a fierce look that had stopped many an angry person in his tracks. His gray eyes twinkled at Angela. "Come here, gal, and sit down. You done walked far enough."

She paused in front of him, and he could see she was upset. Her lips stuck out and her eyes avoided him. He silently asked for the right words to calm her. "Go sit down. You have no business out here. It's too hot for the flies." Buster smiled, held out his right arm and directed her to a wooden patio chair next to the white porch swing. After she sat, he cut a yellow rose from one of his neatly trimmed bushes and handed it to her. "This is for my little flower girl. Now what got you all bothered on this quiet Sunday morning? Where you flying off to?"

Angela took a deep breath, looked up at the tall oak tree and blinked her ebony eyes, "I feel so stupid." Tears fell down her round cheeks. "Everybody must know I'm a fool. I'm going to Danielle's house to talk to her about Pearce. I want to know what's going on between them. Buster, do you know?"

"Dixie Mae," Buster yelled. "Come out here and bring Angela a cold drink." He shook his gray head, "Oh, Lord, have mercy."

A moment later Dixie Mae came out carrying a tray with a pitcher of lemonade and glasses. She poured some for Buster and Angela and sat on the porch step. Her long fingernails matched the pink in her flowered sundress. She wore pink and gold Chinese slippers on her bunioned feet. She threw a damp towel over her thin shoulders and told Angela, "Listen, child, God and the Devil have a lot of things in store for you. It's like a war. You're so young still. Don't use all your energy on the Devil's work. God gave you a special baby." She put her bony hands on Angela's bare shoulders and looked straight into those sad eyes. "And it will always be your job to take care of it. Always!"

Angela set the cold glass down and put her hands on her abdomen. "But you don't know how much I love him. It hurts so bad. Just like somebody died. Even worse than death. I did everything he asked me to."

"Well," Buster smiled and rubbed his balding head, "a man loves a woman who loves him like that."

"Bullshit!" Dixie Mae stood up. "That's the problem, Angela. You been too good to that fool. And the way you're holding your stomach, you better let Pearce take you to the hospital right now. There he is standing down there by the car. Buster, go tell him to come on."

Angela lay shivering under the warm blankets on the cold, hard delivery table. The room was warm, the bright lights blinded her, and Dr. Lee stood in front of the large mirror with his hands on her stomach. He could always make Angela laugh and cheer her up. His radiant smile lit up the room whenever he entered.

Now, Angela saw the seriousness in his dark blue eyes. "Come on, honey, just one more big push and it's all over."

Angela took another deep breath, squeezed her eyes closed and pushed hard. Nothing happened, and Angela screamed with the next overwhelming contraction.

Dr. Lee yelled, "Get surgery on the line, stat! We're not getting full dilation. Order prep for emergency C-section. Get moving!" He snatched his mask off and took Angela's hand, "You're in good hands. You know what's happening here. We're going to get your baby out soon. I promise."

Angela looked frightened. He squeezed her hand again and said, "I know you have a lot of faith. Don't stop now, we're almost at the finish line." He smiled, turned away, ripped off his gown and gloves and raced out the double doors.

Two nurses wheeled Angela's gurney down the busy hallway,

stopping long enough for her to receive hugs from Buster and Dixie Mae. The contractions came faster and harder now. Angela grabbed Buster's hairy arm, "Please make them do something!"

Dixie Mae gave the nurses a puzzled look. The elevator door opened and Angela was wheeled inside. The impatient, red-haired nurse spoke sharply, "We're going down to the operating room and Dr. Lee is going to perform a Cesarean section. We'll let you know when it's all over." She closed the door before they could say another word.

The next afternoon Angela woke up and looked around the beautifully decorated maternity room. The carpet and bedspreads were pale blue like the hearts painted on the soft pink walls. Red shadows of sunset filtered through the white miniblinds and reminded her she had been asleep all day. The other bed, neatly made up, had a mint green teddy bear sitting on the plump pillows. Angela welcomed the solitude. A spicy fragrance of flowers took her attention to a giant bouquet of red and pink roses covering the entire bedside table. A silver greeting card sat next to the flowers. She held her breath, turned very slowly with her hands on her stomach the way the nurses had shown her, picked up the card and read the four words.... "Don't leave me. Pearce"

Angela had not talked to him since he brought her to the hospital yesterday. She remembered she had told Dr. Lee not to let Pearce in the room. The red-haired nurse, Peggy, told her that Pearce had come to look at the baby in the nursery window down the hall. Right now Angela wanted to talk to her mother, Rose, in Los Angeles. This might just be the time to go back home and let Pearce live his life the way he wanted without them. She held the card in one hand and dialed her mother's job at Lady Green's Boutique.

"She's so beautiful, Mama," Angela said. "She weighs seven pounds and she's twenty-one inches long. Her legs are long and fat like mine. Her eyes are big and black like mine. Thick black hair."

"Well, baby, I'm glad you're all right," Rose said. "Angela, you know that damned F.B.I. is still watching my house and they probably have my phone tapped. The same men keep coming by to ask me the same questions. 'Do you know where they're at? You know, Mrs. Adams, if we find them they could be in a lot of trouble. And even though Angela is innocent, she could get hurt. If you hear from them, tell Pearce to give himself up 'cause it's just a matter of time 'til we find him.'

"Same old thing all the time. I told them if they find out where you all are to let me know." Rose continued, "Angela, when you coming home, baby?"

Angela looked at the card in her left hand again. "I just don't know right now, Mama."

Rose went on, "Let Pearce stay if he wants to. It doesn't make any sense to have my only grandchild in all that shit. How's he doing anyway? I told him to call me at my friend's house and let me know as soon as the baby was born."

Angela wanted to tell her mother right then and there that she was coming back home. She looked at the card again. "Pearce is being good to us," she lied. "Mama, the baby looks like him too. She has a wide little nose, a dimple in each cheek and a pretty little heart-shaped mouth." Angela heard her mother's soft sobs through the phone. "Please don't cry, Mama."

Angela continued quietly, "Guess what? She has a rainbow smile just like you. She's so sweet. We named her Candi Rose. I know you have to get off the phone now and yes, I will take good care of her."

She hated lying, but she knew her mother worried about her

and was always telling her to come back and for Pearce to turn himself in. Pearce hated talking to Rose. She was always telling him how to live with his family. Always mixing in their business.

Angela was tired and the pain medication took effect now. She fell asleep and dreamed about Pearce's dancing footsteps and her heart racing. Anger and bitterness kept reminding her that he had been seeing another woman. Those footsteps kept getting closer and closer. Suddenly, she woke up to Pearce's loud, angry voice. "I'm going to see my wife and none of y'all gonna stop me. I did everything for her and now she wants to act stupid."

Angela heard a deep, male voice. "We will escort you from the building. Are you going to leave quietly now?"

Then she heard Pearce answer, "You don't scare me just 'cause you're a security guard, but I'm leaving anyway 'cause I'm tired. I'll see her when I come to take them home and no damn body gonna stop me then."

Angela crept out of bed and held on to the opened door to keep from falling. She decided it would be better for everybody concerned to let Pearce come in. Just as she started to call out to him, a lady stepped over to him from the waiting area. The big hips and the long, sun-streaked auburn hair. Danielle! A green light flashed at the top of the elevator and the door opened. Danielle put her arm around Pearce and the two of them stepped inside.

Angela stood frozen holding on to the door. Peggy rushed to her from the nurses' station. She took Angela's arm and walked her slowly back to bed.

"Look, honey, I don't know what's going on but your husband left this note for you. And you can read it as soon as you lay back down." She helped Angela get into bed, pulled up the cool pink sheet with the soft blue blanket and then handed her the note. "Now read this and don't get up anymore. You have a call light if you need help." She walked back to the door shaking her head. "These young mothers think they know everything," she muttered. She hesitated, looked back at Angela and left the door wide open.

Angela was very tired and welcomed the firm bed. She read the words that put her to sleep..... "I'm sorry I hurt you. The baby is almost as pretty as you are. I know you won't talk to me on the phone. Danielle came to the hospital to speak to you. You promised to always stay with me. I hope you like the roses. Pearce"

The next morning, Angela lay back on the plump pillows and held her soft, warm baby in her arms. She kissed her little wrinkled fingers, thanked God for this bright new day and pushed all sad thoughts from her mind. All she wanted to do was love this precious child forever.

Suddenly, a three-foot, yellow teddy bear with a bright pink ribbon around its neck appeared in the doorway. Pearce stood behind it wearing faded blue jeans and navy blue penny loafers. He peaked around it. His mustache curling over his infectious smile.

"How did you get in here?" Angela's hand went to the call light.

"Wait a minute, baby. Wait—please wait a minute." He hurried over to her and set the teddy bear on the bed and took her hand in his. "How could you refuse this handsome guy? Come on, you know you like yellow." He gathered Candi in his arms and sat in the bedside chair. "Look at those snapping black eyes, Angela. Just like yours."

Angela shifted her body slowly and faced the wall.

Pearce said, "You're gonna talk to me sooner or later, Angela. I'm getting tired of you fooling around. I'm taking you and Candi home tomorrow. That's that."

She turned around quickly, ignoring her post-op pain, and looked at Candi asleep in his arms with her little hand wrapped around his thumb. Then she stared straight into his honey eyes. "Now that's real cute. You are the last person in the world to be telling somebody what the hell to do. I'm not doing anything you tell me anymore, 'cause you don't own me or this baby. You and Danielle can do whatever you want because I don't care at all. I'm going back home to L.A. with my baby."

Pearce's voice softened now. "I can't let you take Candi from me. You know I need both of you. That's the reason I brought you to Georgia, because I didn't want to go to jail and be away from you. I'll do anything you ask me if you stay with me."

He touched the gold wedding band on her left hand. "I'll work it out with the robbery thing. But I can't go back now. You know it was somebody that looked like me. My father was put in jail and they threw away the key. Angela, come home with me at least until you get better and give me a chance. At least let Candi get to know her father. All three of us need a chance together."

"Okay." Angela said softly. "No more staying out late. No more lies and don't even talk to Danielle. Can you do that?" She started to cry.

Pearce placed Candi on the bed and held Angela in his arms. "Don't cry, baby. We'll work it out this time."

Angela wrapped her fingers in his soft curls and kissed him on the lips. He lifted her hair off her shoulder, kissed her neck and laid his head on her full breasts.

For the next six weeks Pearce was an absolute angel. He came right home after his job as a desk clerk at the Holiday Inn. He had let his beard grow, and his hair was past shoulder length now. He dared anyone to recognize him. He told Angela that Danielle had moved out of town and there was nothing to it anyway. Angela had a little trouble believing him but she enjoyed all his attention.

During the day, Buster came to visit and Dixie Mae took care of Candi just as she did all the little babies on Park Lane.

Between Dixie Mae in the day and Pearce at night, practically all Angela could do for Candi was to breastfeed her. But everyone was happy and she knew she had the rest of her life to love this child. And having Dixie Mae around kept her from missing her mother, Rose, so much.

Angela stepped out of the warm shower, closed her eyes and enjoyed the cool night breeze from the open window caressing her wet skin. She heard the stereo playing "Let's Stay Together" by Al Green, their favorite song. Pearce had the lights dimmed. He took her by the hand and led her to the bed. "Come here, sit down, baby, and let me rub some warm lotion on you. I know how tired you are after a long day with Candi. She's asleep now, so you don't have to take care of anybody but me," he smiled. He put lotion on her shoulders and started to remove her towel.

"No!" She got up and stood at the open window. "I can't. I still can't forget about you and Danielle." Angela stuck out her lips in a pout and closed her eyes.

Pearce said, "Don't say that ugly bitch's name to me. She tried her best to break us up. Kept flirting with me, but she can't compare to you, baby. I wouldn't want anybody but my ebony-eyed sugar." He pulled the blue satin curtain back from the window. "Smell those lilacs, baby. Just like you. Come on, sit next to me for a minute." He patted the bed and Angela sat. He looked into her eyes and said, "You need this, baby."

He laid her slowly down on the bed, stretching her arms straight out over her head until her fingertips touched the cool wall behind her. She felt his warm kisses from her face to her breast. Then his tongue trailed down to her right thigh, where he bit her softly. She took his face in her hands and put her warm tongue on his.

Pearce threw on his white tank top and brushed his hair. He turned around, looked at Angela sleeping and sat next to her. He ran his hand up and down her thigh, then he picked her foot up and bit her softly on the leg. She woke up and smiled at him.

Pearce said, "I'm going to the store to get some cigarettes, baby. I'll be right back."

He danced down the narrow walkway onto the lane and took a deep breath of cool evening air and felt free and alive. A pair of lightning bugs flickered beside him and echoed the freedom in his soul. He walked along in the shadows of the tall elm trees and felt equal to any free man out of jail. He passed Buster and Dixie Mae sitting in the old porch swing. "Good evening, ma'am, good evening, sir." He flashed them his infectious smile.

"How's your job?" Dixie Mae's voice rang out in between the squeaks of the swing.

"Just fine, real busy." Pearce went on with his hands in his pockets. "Nosey old biddies," he said under his breath. "Country folks sure are nosey."

He stepped into the brightly lit convenience store and greeted the familiar clerk behind the counter, "What's going on, Tony?"

"Nothing but the heat. What you need, Pearce?"

"Pack of Winstons. And gimme a black pair of those fuzzy dice that you hang on the car mirror."

Tony placed them in a brown bag with the cigarettes. "Some folks say these things bring you luck."

Pearce handed him a five, dropped the change into the Sickle Cell collection box and carried his prize in the moonlight. The whole lane was quiet except for Dixie Mae's squeaky swing. He smiled again at the old biddies, stopped by his Chevy, tossed the dice into the glove compartment and locked the door. Then he nodded his head, smiling. "Now ain't Danielle gonna love these hanging in her new Cadillac."

Chapter 3

September came and brought cool, moist winds to Valdosta. The golden noonday sun gleamed through red and yellow oak leaves, lighting up a mixture of brown beer bottles and wayward cigarette butts on the crooked sidewalk outside of Red Jake's Pool Hall.

Pearce sat in his Chevy and watched Jake clean up this spot on Clay Street, two blocks from Park Lane on the south side of town. School children crossed the street with a wrinkled, dark-skinned guard. The small church on the corner, Mt. Zion Temple, looked deserted. Tall, yellow sunflowers stood on both sides of the entrance, swaying in the soft breeze.

Pearce breathed deeply and sighed. He had to walk past Red Jake before going next door into Danielle's Beauty Nook. He got out of the car with a large brown envelope and approached Jake, giving him his infectious smile. The tan, freckled man wore khaki trousers rolled up to his fat knees. His large muscles flexed in a rapid rhythm under a white tank top while he swept the area.

Pearce wondered why this bald-headed man cleaned up the same mess every day at the same time, only to have it return when the daily crowd of pool hustlers came on the scene. "I'm not getting in anybody's rut," he said to himself, squinting his eyes from the blinding sun. "Hey, Jake, what's the number today? I know you hit the big one," Pearce said.

Red Jake leaned on the push broom, his plump, pink lips smiling. "Let me tell you a secret, Pearce," his face got serious. "You know that sign in the window that says 'Gone Fishing'? When I hit the big one, you're gonna see it, but it's just gonna say 'Gone.'" His wide belly shook with laughter under a brown snakeskin belt. "I don't know what number came in this morning, but it sure wasn't mine."

Pearce gave him a high five and they laughed together. He liked Red Jake, but he believed in making his own luck. He also believed he could control his destiny by staying out of jail.

The sweet fragrance of jasmine shampoo and hot curling irons greeted Pearce before he opened the back door to Danielle's Beauty Nook. He pushed the hanging black-and-white beads aside and walked right through. The stereo played "Georgia on My Mind," a mellow tune by Ray Charles, and the small portable television had a long-legged patron, Kartina, entranced with the noontime soap operas.

Danielle placed the last huge pink roller in Kartina's black, waist-length hair. Pearce crept up behind her, put his hands on her wide hips and kissed her on the side of her caramel-colored neck. She turned around and slapped him playfully but firmly on his curly, brown head. "Get outta here, fool. I told you I don't have time for you. I'm busy and you ought to be too." She shook her head, swinging her long, red hair, and escorted Kartina to the dryer next to a giant black and gold artificial plant. She made her comfortable with a footstool for her long legs and a stack of magazines and set a gold tray with iced tea beside her.

Pearce sat in a chair, swung around facing the gold-leaf mirror and slid a tiny comb through his silky mustache. "You know I'm on my lunch break and I came by to bring you something." He looked at her sparkling, hazel eyes, her heart-shaped mouth and knew he wanted to spend the rest of the day with her. "But, if you don't want it, I'll go over to Red Jake's, grab me a chicken sandwich and get back to work."

He started for the door but she gently grabbed his white shirtsleeve, stopping him. Her face lit up with a shy smile, "Well...tell me what is it."

Pearce glanced at his bag and took her hand in his. Looking into her eyes, he said softly, "Come go with me now, Danielle."

She sighed, slipped on her red heels and gave Shirley, her shampoo girl, a knowing look. Pearce held the door open, smiled, bowed and extended his hand, "After you, Madame." He turned his head quickly, looked again at Kartina's long legs, blew a kiss her way and gave her a promising wink.

Pearce sat with Danielle on the black velvet seats in her cranberry-red Cadillac at Nash's fishing hole, looking at the reflection of the moonlight on the dark blue water. They had spent the afternoon in her lavish apartment but he had not yet shown her the contents of the envelope. He took a deep breath and began, "Danielle, there's a lot of things you don't know about me." He held her soft hands in both of his. Fireflies flickered around the low brush and crickets chirped their evening songs in the stillness.

"Pearce, just show me what's in the bag. Wait!" She placed her hand over his, holding the bag. "If it's dope, forget it." She gave him a stern look.

"Aw, shit!" he spat out. "Why would I want to give you some dope? You know I ain't into that." He put the bag on the other side of him by the door.

Danielle reached over him to get it, "Give it here!"

Pearce shoved it into his shirt pocket, hurried out of the car, slammed the door and sat on the damp, red dirt. Danielle followed him quickly and stood over him with her hands on her hips, "Show it to me or I'm getting in my car and leaving your ass here."

Pearce pulled out a pack of cigarettes, "Aw, shit! I left my lighter somewhere." He smiled at her angry face. "You got a match?" He leaned back on the cool sand. Danielle walked swiftly back to her car. Pearce jumped up, grabbing her arm before she opened the door. "Okay, come back here. I'll show you. I'll show you! Here."

He handed her the bag and helped her sit on the bank. Danielle opened the bag, took out a worn, eight-by-ten photo, unfolded it and smoothed out the creases.

Pearce began, "This is my family. Ain't seen them in almost two years. This is my twin brother, Paul. He got killed in a car accident. I didn't even go to the funeral."

He saw the puzzled look on Danielle's face. She lit his cigarette for him and he went on talking. "I'm a fugitive. The Feds want me in L.A."

"That's why you wouldn't let me shave your beard!"

"Some guys I hung around with pulled a robbery and somebody put the finger on me. My family raised the bail money, and right after that I left the state. My brother drove me to the train station. Gave me every dime he had. I never saw him again."

Danielle placed her hand on his bare shoulder. "Why didn't you go back to the funeral if you two were so close?"

"Look," Pearce said, pointing to the older female in the photo. "This is my mother. She did everything she could for us after my father went to jail. She begged me not to come home because she knew the police would expect me to be there. Said to remember Paul like he was the last time I saw him. She had my sister and my older brother to look after her and I knew she would be all right."

Danielle's voice rose and her eyes got wide. "Angela came all the way down here away from her family with you just because you said you didn't do it?"

"I didn't do anything!"

"All I can say is she must really love you." She shook her head. "And you're not going back to straighten things out?"

"Angela thinks she loves me but she don't know nothing about me." He looked at Danielle curiously. "You don't believe me, do you?"

"I don't know right now, Pearce, but it's getting late. Angela must be worried by now. Let me take you back." She stood up.

Suddenly, he hated himself for confiding in her and he shook his head. "You don't know if you believe me right now? You should be able to say yes or no right now and if you can't then I don't need you for nothing. Or Angela either. Leave me alone."

"Pearce, I'm sorry about what happened to your brother."

"No, you're not. Get out of here. I don't need you."

Danielle stood up, took three steps towards the car, turned around and said, "I could help you if you want to go back and fight it."

"You can't help me do shit," he screamed at her. "Go on, just get the fuck out of here! I don't want to see you anymore. Just disappear! Bitch!"

She stood there with her mouth open, ready to say something, but she shook her head and hurried to her car. After she got in and started the engine, she rolled the window down and shouted at him as loud as she could, "You look like a faggot with that ugly-ass beard. Good-bye!"

He turned his back to her and started to throw stones into the murky water as far as he could. "Women, women, women! Fuck 'em all." Always trying to run his life, doubting him. "Who needs 'em!" He turned briefly at the sound of Danielle's Cadillac racing out over the stony dirt.

Pearce folded his arms behind his curly head and lay back on the sand, feeling the cool pebbles on his bare shoulders. He gazed far into the night. The biggest and brightest stars he had ever seen kissed the dark sky. He strained his eyes and looked way up to the tiny, tiny ones millions of miles away. He closed his honey eyes and listened to the tall elm trees swaying in the easy wind. His body relaxed in the fresh air, almost asleep.

Pearce jumped when an elderly gentleman threw his fishing line into the still water. He sat up quickly and tossed some more stones into the water. He watched the ripples come closer and closer, beckoning him. He stood and eased his feet into the lukewarm, slimy pond. A wrinkled, brown newspaper floated towards him, stopping at his hairy leg. Pearce picked it up, shaking the water off, and read it in the moonlight. The train to Chicago. Leaving at midnight.

He thought of all the women who could destroy him at any given moment. Angela, Danielle and his own mother. Now even his little daughter, Candi.

He read the ad again. Maybe a good idea. He had ridden the midnight train to Georgia. His life was like the stone he held in his left hand. Not big enough to count by itself, but small enough to go alone. Pearce folded the newspaper, stuffed it into his Levis, put on his shoes and headed towards the quiet street.

Angela placed the light yellow blanket over Candi before looking out the screen door again. The midnight breeze chilled her but did nothing to ease her anxiety. Pearce had not come home after work as he always did, and Angela had called the hotel hours ago. The manager said he went out on an errand. She dared not try again, knowing they frowned on personal calls. She hadn't heard from him since his lunch hour when he said he'd be home after four o'clock.

Now she thought something had gone wrong. Perhaps he had been captured by the F.B.I. Maybe he had tried to run away from them. Or even been killed. He told her he would die before he spent one day locked up. The only thing she knew was to wait. Candi slept peacefully in her crib. Pink ribbons on her thick braids. Her thumb in her mouth.

Angela couldn't believe more than a year had passed since they had brought this exact replica of herself home. Pearce had been good to them, giving them everything except a life with her relatives in California. Angela had made a few friends, but none knew the real reason she and Pearce had come to Georgia.

Now, she fretted. She held Candi's soft little hand, kissed it until warm tears fell down her face. "Oh, God, what am I going to do?" Angela could almost hear her mother's firm voice break through the silence. "There's only one thing to do when you got problems, child. Doctors can't give you nothing for it. Get down on your knees and pray. Let God show you the way."

Candi turned over in her crib and Angela let go of her hand and switched the lamp off, letting the silver moonlight bathe the silent room. She kneeled down with her head on her arms in the overstuffed side chair. She prayed helplessly with salty tears washing her face. "Please send him home," she begged.

Candi climbed out of her crib and into the chair above Angela. Angela felt her presence but kept on asking God to send her husband home. Candi sat with her little feet on Angela's shoulders, stuck her thumb back in her mouth and went back to sleep.

Angela got up, returning Candi to her bed. Exhausted now, she finally lay down on top of the cool, rayon bedspread. She drifted into a restless sleep, when suddenly she heard Candi jump up and down in her bed and shriek with laughter. Angela looked up. Pearce stood in the doorway playing peek-a-boo with Candi.

Angela stared at him. He didn't say a word. He just picked up the baby and walked into the kitchen.

"What's for dinner, baby? I'm starving. I could eat a horse. I felt so bad this afternoon. It must have been that nasty lunch they served at work today. I went into one of the empty rooms and fell asleep on the bed. When I woke up it was twelve o'clock. I came right home 'cause I knew you were probably worried. Were you?" He looked at her with threatening eyes.

"Just a little bit, honey," Angela lied forcing a nervous smile. "But I knew you had a good reason."

Pearce always became agitated when she told him she worried about him. He kept reminding her that he wasn't going back to L.A. and she just better put it out of her mind. He sat at the table, held Candi in his lap while Angela took a green salad out of the refrigerator.

He stood up and sat the baby in her high chair with a strawberry popsicle.

He walked over to Angela and wrapped his arms around her slender waist. "Look, baby, you know I love you and nothing is going to keep me away from my two girls."

Angela turned away to go to the sink, hiding the tears in her eyes. Pearce put his hands on her waist, turning her around, holding her tight, kissing her face, her ears and her neck. That night Angela forgot all about his being late. Temporarily.

Chapter 4

"Ain't no damn gold in Georgia! They dug all that shit up years ago. And if you wasn't there, you didn't get none. Buster, I say, for an old man you sure got a lot of dreams," Red Jake looked at his old friend and shook his balding head.

Buster rested his skinny rake on his porch steps and eased his body down beside Jake. "A lot of folks think I'm crazy, but you been knowing me for a long time and you know how I loved my mama. Told me on her dying bed that this property was hers. Left to her by old man Finch. Said he gave her the land from Park Lane to Ruby Street. When old man Finch lay sick and dying, everybody deserted him but my mama. She took care of him 'til the end.

"He wrote it down and the papers are here somewhere. There's some gold 'round here too. When I find the papers, I find the gold."

"I don't know about that, Buster," Jake scratched his head and smiled. "But I know your mama took care of folks when nobody else would. I remember that time she bought me some tennis shoes. I didn't ask her for them. She said she wanted me to be like the rest of the kids on the first day of school. She said I was worth it and she knew I would do good that year."

"Yeah, motherfucker, you got better grades than I did." Buster playfully punched Jake on the shoulder. "But I didn't know it was because of those shoes, man."

"Buster, nobody knew she bought 'em. She said tell everybody I worked and got 'em myself. She treated me better than my own family. They really didn't have time for me, but Miss Sarah did."

Old Buster picked up his fork and cut another chunk of sweet, red watermelon. Then he returned to his chore of raking the crispy autumn leaves, while the sun beamed stronger as sweat bathed his bushy eyebrows.

"You know she loved all folks, and kids most of all. She told me to care for all of them on this lane." Buster clinched his fists. "I just have to find them papers, by God, I have to! I been looking for two years now. Jake, you know my mama was for real. Just as real as that little gal running down here to get in my way."

Candi wore pink shorts and a white pinafore blouse that showed her tummy. Neat braids stuck up in the air with long, white ribbons that bounced on her shoulders as she ran straight into Buster's big hands. He lifted her way over his head, looking into her shining black eyes and at that crooked smile. He held her close and stood her firmly on the grass. "Good morning, little lady. How come you not helping your mama in her yard?" He returned Angela's smile with a wave.

Candi jumped right into Buster's tidy mound of leaves, and with the help of the slight wind scattered them everywhere. She threw them up in the air, giggling when they fell down around her, some landing in her hair. She laughed so hard it was as if someone held her tight and tickled her. Buster tried to be upset and Red Jake hid the smirk on his face but his wide belly shook, giving him away.

Buster wiped his eyebrows, smiled, found a yellow can with a spout and handed it to Candi. "Here, busy little lady, go water them tomatoes 'long side the fence."

Candi began soaking the soil and stomped in the mud with her white tennis shoes. Jake helped Buster finish picking up the leaves.

"Buster, hurry up and let's go fishing. At least we know it's some catfish around here. I still say, there ain't no gold in Georgia. But I'll help you find the papers for this land. What you gon' do if you find 'em?"

"I'm gonna tear down all these old houses and build some decent places for folks to stay in and be proud. Then I'm gonna build a sports center in honor of my mother, Sarah B. Jenkins." He smiled, looking down the street as if he could see it on the corner where the Satin Slipper stood.

Jake turned to Candi. "Look at that child, now she got your fork digging in the dirt."

"Yeah," Buster said, "she workin' hard like she diggin' for gold!" Buster and Jake looked at each other wide-eyed.

Angela enrolled in Valdosta Junior College in a paralegal program. She believed that one day Pearce would not be around to take care of her and Candi. Pearce objected at first but finally agreed, thinking that she would have something to do other than to keep pushing him to turn himself in.

Angela walked out of the busy classroom one evening and found a handsome white man waiting for her. He extended his hand and shook hers firmly. "Hi Angela, I'm Carl Finch. The instructor next door."

He had caught her off-guard, sending electricity right through her. His spicy cologne and sea-green eyes mesmerized her. He wore a black-and-white pinstriped three-piece suit. About six feet tall, brown freckles on a sunburned nose. His chestnut hair with just a hint of gray at the temples rested on his broad shoulders. His white silk shirt opened at the collar to show matching hair on his chest.

Angela's voice shook, "You know my name?"

"Yes, I've been watching you for a long time. You seem so serious about your studies. We need more students like you around here."

Angela felt a surge of unexplained chemistry between them. She avoided those calm eyes that twinkled and looked right at hers. "I'm serious, but I really enjoy the program." She hugged her books and smiled shyly. "Well, it was nice meeting you." She turned to walk away.

"Wait, Angela, here's my card. Call me." Carl walked away, leaving her to read the card, which said "Carl Finch, Attorney at Law."

He took a few steps and came back to her. "You know, Angela, you have the brightest smile." He shook her hand again. "You might need a friend, Cookie."

He hurried down the crowded hallway and out the double doors. She stood watching him. He stopped on the top step at the exit, waved and gave her a big smile and a salute.

"Cookie?" Angela said to herself and smiled before she came down to Earth and began looking around for Pearce. Not here yet. She walked out the exit to a trash bin, looked at the card again and tossed it away. "No way. A white man. I can't get involved."

She sat on the steps and waited for her husband. Thirty minutes passed and no Pearce. She closed her textbook, stood up, went back to the trashcan and retrieved the business card, remembering his words, "You might need a friend."

Suddenly, she heard running footsteps from behind. "Hey, baby, don't be upset. I had a flat tire on the way. You know how that car is sometimes," Pearce said.

Angela jumped, startled by his appearance, then she remembered her disgust at his frequent tardiness and walked to the old Chevy, not saying a word. She slipped the card into her skirt pocket.

Candi climbed into the front seat on Angela's lap and gave her a big kiss. "Mommie."

Angela hugged her and returned the kiss. Pearce looked straight ahead to the winding road. "Baby, after I take you and Candi home I have to go buy a new set of tires."

"Honey, we don't mind going with you. We really don't see

that much of you. Besides we need to catch up on some things," Angela said, touching his arm and smiling.

"That shop ain't no place for my two girls to be hanging around. Too many greasy old men." Pearce turned the corner and parked in front of the duplex on Park Lane. "I'll be back soon. Wait up for me." He pinched her thigh before she took the baby inside.

Angela settled down for the night. She opened her textbook and took the card out of her pocket. Cookie. Why did he call me Cookie? He must know that I'm married. He had to see my wedding rings. Carl Finch Jr. Finch.

Sounds familiar. She sighed and put the card away and checked the time. It's after eleven. Pearce isn't back yet. Four hours to get a new set of tires? Angela ate a bowl of chicken soup and some of Dixie Mae's peach cobbler with French vanilla ice cream and went to bed. Alone.

After three weeks of passing Carl in the hallway between classes, Angela agreed to meet him for dinner at the Royal Coach Inn, an exclusive restaurant on the north side of Valdosta. Shrimp cocktails preceded juicy lobster tails, filet mignon and Caesar salad. Was it the sparkling red wine or his calm sea-green eyes making her feel lightheaded?

"Tell me, Carl," she smiled, "why did you call me 'Cookie' the day you met me?"

"You remind me of someone I used to know. A very kind, old black woman. She cared for my grandfather during his last days on Earth. We called her 'Cookie' because she fed us such delectable meals. My grandfather was undeniably an ornery old cuss. He let nothing stand in the way of what he wanted. Cookie always came by the house to see about him."

Carl buttered a piece of bread and handed it to her, smiling. "That woman's eyes lit up like the stars when she smiled. And they were dark, dark. Like yours."

He took a yellow rose from the crystal vase, touched her nose with it and handed it to her. "For my friend."

Angela rubbed the soft, sweet petals under her nose and tears came into her eyes. "I shouldn't be here. I...."

Carl reached over the table, squeezed her hand and said slowly, "I hope I haven't offended you. I just want your company. That's all. Well, I like you too, and I want to see you again. But that," he smiled, "is up to you."

Angela took a deep breath, blew it out and blinked her eyes. Candi was waiting for her at home. She stood up, "I have to go now."

He stood up, hugged her briefly and planted a quick kiss on her cheek. He sat back down quietly. Angela hurried out the door.

Angela decided that being with Carl every now and then would only help her accept the fact that Pearce could not be depended on anymore. Maybe a friend could keep her from worrying about him. Carl needed her for companionship since he was divorced with grown children who moved away a long time ago. He always spoke kind words to her, asking nothing of her but company. And since Buster and Dixie Mae practically adopted Candi as their own child, they encouraged her to go out and leave her with them. Sometimes she caught the bus to meet Carl or walked to his regional office, which was close to her school. When she was pregnant with Candi, she rode in a taxi driven by a man named Weldon, who liked her and told her whenever she needed a ride to call him. He never charged her, but he liked to flirt and that was all it ever was.

Carl showed Angela new and exciting places and assisted her with the tedious paralegal studies. They went roller-skating, to lectures and even on nature walks through the forests. This clear, balmy night, they went to Cocono Beach on the outskirts of Valdosta. They sat on a white blanket on the soft amber sand. The moon cast its full silver shadow on the dark, restless sea. This section of the beach was quiet and deserted except for the sound of billowing white waves and a tired beach bum walking out of sight, leaving the two of them to their picnic. Carl uncorked the sparkling champagne, startling the sea gulls, sending them flapping their wings and squawking away.

Carl clinked his glass with Angela's. "A toast to our friendship. May it last forever."

Angela set the crystal goblet on the blanket. "Carl, don't you have any problems being with a black woman?"

"Of course I think about it a great deal and I know some people would certainly frown upon it, but I like you. What can I say? You're always smiling and I forget about things like color difference."

Angela sat Indian style with her elbows on her knees. "There is so much you don't know about me. So many things that I've been through."

"You don't have to tell me anything you don't want to." He moved next to her, twisted her long hair in his hands, kissed the back of her neck and touched her cameo earrings. "How do you take these things off?"

"Why? You want one?" she teased.

"No," he sighed, "I want to kiss your ears." He held her face in his hands, kissed her ears, her eyelids and whispered, "I want all of my Cookie."

Angela became entranced. Her breath came faster and faster. She broke away from his embrace. "Carl, things are happening too fast." Then she laid her head on his warm chest. She felt his heart pounding.

"Angela, I'll go as fast as you want or as slow as you want."

Angela said, just above a whisper, "I want to."

"I know you do. I can tell that." He took her hand and placed her index finger in the sand, making a wide circle. Inside he wrote, "Carl and Cookie, best friends."

"You're so sweet." She smiled, "What am I going to do with you?"

"I don't know but somebody's got sand all over your pretty legs." His eyes twinkled. He leaned his head down blowing it off. "Here's some more." He kept blowing all the way to her knees. He slid her skirt up, now planting warm kisses on her shivering thighs. Angela lay motionless until his lips reached her red silk panties.

"Wait." She pushed him away. "Stop a minute. Let me think about what I'm doing here." She stood up and brushed the sand off of her. "Don't you move one bit."

He sat still and quiet on the blanket with his hands on his lap. She sat beside him again. "Who told you that you could do all that stuff to me?" She pushed him gently over onto the sand and lay down on top of him. She held him and dug her fingers into his back while he kissed her neck and softly touched her breasts.

"Carl," she said when she found her voice again and looked into his eyes, "I want you inside me."

Angela returned home late that night thinking about Carl's lips on her thighs. Nobody's here. Pearce must not have picked up Candi from Buster's. She looked into the mirror beaming, smiling and thinking about her outing with Carl. She turned around and around in joy. She realized she felt happy for the first time in years. The panda-shaped night-light caught her attention and right beside it lay Candi's stray white sock. Angela picked it up, opened the drawer that she shared with her. The rest of Candi's socks were missing too. That's strange. What happened? She opened the next drawer slowly. Empty. Then each one of the rest quickly. All of the baby's things were gone. "Oh, God, what's going on?" She spun around to the closet. Pearce and Candi's clothes were missing.

Buster turned off the water hose and headed for his screen door. He saw Angela running towards him. "Oh, Lord, what's wrong now?" he said.

"Buster," Angela said out of breath, "they're gone. Where did they go? Everything's gone. All the clothes. What happened? My baby's gone. Where did they go?"

Buster held on to Angela and yelled, "Dixie Mae, Dixie Mae! Come out here!"

Dixie Mae came rushing from the house and they all went back to Angela's.

"He picked her up an hour ago. He said everything was okay." Dixie Mae explained.

"Yeah," Buster added, looking at Dixie Mae, "'cause you asked him. Said he was acting all nervous."

Dixie Mae sat down on the double bed. "Listen, Angela, you have to call the police. They'll find 'em. They can't be that far."

"No! No! No! No police." Then Angela's voice softened when Dixie Mae began sobbing in Buster's arms. "Candi might be frightened. He won't hurt her."

Dixie Mae stood up and wiped her eyes, "Why would he do that to you anyway? Why would he take her?"

Angela shook her head. "He was always whining about his daddy leaving him. He said he would never leave Candi without a father. I don't know why he does what he does, but I gotta have my baby back."

Dixie Mae sighed, "Maybe he left a note."

They began a search around the small duplex. Buster and Dixie Mae met up with Angela in the bathroom. She sat on the bathtub holding a piece of yellowed newspaper.

"What's that?" said Buster.

Angela's voice trembled. "He can't be going there."

Buster grabbed the paper. He and Dixie Mae read it together. "Catch the midnight train to Chicago. Tickets available at the station."

The three of them got inside of Buster's Buick and he pushed the accelerator to the floor. "Fifteen minutes before the train pulls out. We can make it. Let's just hope that sucker's late tonight." The streets deserted. All green lights. They arrived at the station. No train in sight. They jumped out of the car and raced into the station. The big black-and-white clock said eleven fifty-five. Only a bored looking clerk sat behind the counter, thumbing through a tired issue of *Life* magazine.

Angela, Buster and Dixie Mae hurried to the counter. Buster spoke first, "Excuse me, did the train to Chicago come in yet?"

"Yes sir," the clerk answered in a slow Georgia drawl. "It came and went. Wasn't but two to get on tonight."

Angela said, "Was it a black man with a little girl?"

The clerk squinted his eyes as if in deep thought, rubbed his hairy chin, looked at each one of them in turn and said slowly, "Maybe they did and maybe they didn't. It's not my job to keep up with who comes and goes. Just sell tickets. How many y'all want an where y'all want to go?"

Buster grabbed him by his starched shirt collar. "You answer the lady's question or you will be going to Chicago and you won't need no ticket." His voice echoed throughout the silent station.

Buster let go. The clerk straightened his collar, glanced around the station and said no more.

"Angela, show him the picture," Dixie Mae prompted her with an elbow.

The clerk smiled, his face having returned from beet red to a more natural pink. He looked at Buster, "Yep, that's the pretty little gal. That's them big black eyes." He turned back to

Angela, "He steal her from you? I can't stop the train but I can call the law."

Buster and Dixie looked at Angela.

"No."

The clerk, now eager to help, continued, "Next stop is Waycross. They have to wait twenty minutes for the soldiers from Marshall Field. You can catch them if you hurry."

The trio rushed to the exit. He yelled after them, "Take the south exit off the highway. The north exit is blocked off!"

Buster cursed the heavy traffic. Where's everybody going this time of night? They crept through the congestion at the south exit for what seemed like an eternity. The narrow highway looked like a circus, with white headlights coming from one direction and red taillights lined up in front of them. Tall oak trees bordered the road and stood in back of high, brown light poles. Buster looked at Angela and figured she was praying to herself, and Dixie Mae prayed out loud.

Buster wondered what he would say to Pearce if they found him and Candi. If need be, he would have to whip that mother-fucker's ass to get Candi back for Angela. He mentally prepared himself, tried to contain his anger and prayed a little as well. Praying is fine but sometimes you got to help it along with a little action. Yep, he thought to himself, a little action might help things along.

Finally, the Buick braked at the station in Waycross. The enormous red and black locomotive stood there revving its powerful engine. Black and gray smoke floated from the rear, and the tart smell of diesel filled the night air. They could barely make out Pearce from a side window.

Angela jumped out of the car and raced towards the train. She was halfway there when it pulled out. "Stop! Stop!" waving her arms, but the train kept on down the steel tracks until it was out of sight. Too late.

Buster watched Angela go and sit quietly on the wooden passenger bench and put her face down in her hands. He and Dixie Mae sat beside her, neither of them saying a word. Angela kept her face down in her hands. Quiet.

Suddenly a voice coming from the entrance of the station broke the silence. "Any of y'all folks know this little gal?" A dark brown, middle-aged porter stood there holding Candi's hand. He had a small suitcase in the other hand.

Angela looked up as Candi ran to her. She grabbed her daughter and held her tight while she sobbed with joy. Buster and Dixie Mae looked at the beaming porter with questioning faces.

"Well. I guess you all know her. A man said he was her daddy left her here with a note saying give her to her mama. Said this trip would be too long for her." They all thanked the porter and Angela let go of Candi for a short time so Buster and Dixie Mae could hug her.

Chapter 5

Six months passed and Angela had not heard anything from Pearce. She decided to remain in
Valdosta, finish her studies and earn her certifi-
cate. Carl was still very attentive, offering her a whole new life.
Angela depended on him for love, kindness and companionship. She had a hard time believing Pearce would not even call
at least to talk to Candi. She knew his freedom was more important to him than anything or anybody in the world, but deep
down inside Angela expected Pearce to show up at any time. She
prayed for her absent husband's safety and hoped one day he
would turn himself in. Angela never told any of her new friends,
Dixie Mae, Buster or even Carl—throughout all their passionate
moments—that Pearce was and still is a fugitive. Rose, Angela's
mother, promised to pay her and Candi a visit and meet the people that had been so good to them.

Angela knew Rose was really coming to convince her to go
back home. To provide a living as a single parent, Angela
worked as a clerk for one of Carl's associates. Angela had to tell
Carl what she suspected now. All the signs and symptoms were
there. Nausea and dizziness just like when she was pregnant
with Candi. Yet, she wouldn't know for sure until the appoint-
ment with Dr. Lee in two days. It had to be stress from
everything that happened during the last six months. She prayed
that being pregnant was not the answer. She had to tell Carl anyway. He would understand because he understood everything.
Angela reached him at the corporate office in Atlanta. "Carl, I
need to see you real soon. We have to talk about something."

"Is it your husband? He's contacted you?"

"Carl, please wait a minute," she sighed. "This involves me and you personally." Angela started sobbing.

After a short silence, Carl spoke. "Okay, I guess I can wait 'til I see you. Whatever it is, we can work it out together. Oh, babe, I wish I could be with you right now to hold you. Stop crying and give me a big smile. Come on, Cookie, you can do it."

Angela could never resist smiling when he called her "Cookie." She managed a soft giggle. "I do feel better, but I'll be much better when I see you, sweetie."

"Okay, babe, can you get to the airport tomorrow to meet me? I have a big surprise for you anyway."

"You know I'll be there. I can't wait to see you, sweetie."

"Angela, I want you to close your eyes and put your finger on your lips. Are you doing that?"

Angela felt silly but she answered with a "yes" between puckered lips.

"Okay, that's me kissing my Cookie goodnight. Now go to sleep and have your gorgeous body at the airport."

The next evening at the airport Angela looked at the clock in the busy lobby. Finally, Carl's flight was announced for arrival. She smoothed her hair in place for the tenth time since she left the beauty shop. She felt a little faint but she knew she looked super. She wore a white lace dress and sprayed on the French perfume he had given her after their first night together. She rushed to the gate to wait for him. She felt like a teenager on a first date. She couldn't wait to squeeze him tight. She composed herself and stood patiently while the other passengers walked down the long ramp. "Come on, Carl," she said to herself.

The last person came down, but no Carl. The flight attendants went back inside and closed the door behind them. Maybe he missed the flight. Angela hurried to the counter to check the passenger schedule. His name was not on it. She took a deep breath, "Okay, don't panic. Call the corporate office. Something had to happen." Angela composed herself, walked to the phone, double-checking the information on her notepad. She dialed the office. "Hello, Praline, this is Angela Jones. I'm sorry to bother you, but I need to speak to Carl."

Angela didn't like telling their personal business to his secretary, but this would have to be an exception. Angela continued, "Oh, he's not in? Actually, I was expecting him at the airport in Valdosta, tonight." She heard a long sigh from the other end of the line, then the slow southern drawl, "Angela, Carl must have crossed his dates up somehow. He had a conference in Seattle, Washington. He's due back in two weeks. All I can do is give him a message for you," Praline answered.

Angela went on, "Was this a last-minute thing? Did he just find out this morning?"

"Well, no. Mr. Finch called me today to make reservations for him. I'm sure he just decided last night to attend."

Angela hung up the phone, not knowing what else to do, fought back tears in her eyes, walked quickly out of the lobby and went home. She sat in the corner of the bedroom on the floor, hurt and exhausted.

She heard Buster's loud voice all the way from outside the front door. "Angela, open the door!" She had heard him knocking but she wanted to be alone now though she knew Buster and Dixie Mae were outside worrying. Carl had always been there when she needed him. How could he do this to her? Angela wanted to stay right here in the corner. Please everyone go away. To add to her misery right now she felt the familiar monthly cramping. At least she didn't have to go see Dr. Lee, not for pregnancy anyway.

Dixie Mae sang out to her, "Candi is crying for you. She needs her mama. Come open the door so she can see you are all right. We won't bother you. Just let the baby in. We'll come back and talk when you want to."

Angela stood and walked through the living room to the front door. She knew they saw her shadow from the window because they suddenly stopped pleading with her. She unfastened the chain lock, then quickly fastened it again. "No," she yelled through the door. "Take her away. Everybody leave me alone. Please, I'm okay. Go away, please!"

Angela turned and started walking back to her corner when she heard Buster say, "She's in there all right. Just walked to the door, started to open it and changed her mind. Can't nobody get her out."

Angela froze, afraid to breathe. She heard another voice. It can't be. Mama?

"Angela, open this fucking door now!" It really was her mama, Rose, from Los Angeles. Angela didn't know she was coming now. Angela took a deep breath and opened the door. Rose stood there with steady hands on her ample hips. Her silver-gray hair twisted in a big knot. Her dark black eyes misting. She had moist, caramel skin like Angela's. Her prominent cheekbones softened by a cranberry, heart-shaped mouth. Angela smelled the gardenia cologne as Rose's arms engulfed her.

"Mama, Mama. I didn't want you to see me like this," Angela cried as they held each other. They both continued crying and Rose led Angela to the vinyl sofa. She put Angela's head down on her lap and rubbed her head.

After a few moments of this, Rose kicked off her black lizard-skin pumps and said, "Okay, that's enough of this boohooing."

She straightened Angela up and wiped her face with her lace handkerchief. "Now, start from the beginning and tell me what the hell is going on."

Chapter 6

*B*uster sat his robust frame on the old porch swing, serenaded by the rhythmic squeaks of the rusted hinges. His eyes fixed on the corner where the Satin Slipper nightclub stood. He watched neighborhood teenagers, knowing they were under age, strut proudly through the swinging doors past the unscrupulous doorman. Buster knew somehow something better was in store for that corner. Like the sports center he wanted to build. Lord knows he searched everywhere for the papers to this land. He stood and slapped his daily newspaper against the swing. "And I'm gonna find 'em, damn it!" He slapped the paper again and again, "Damn it! Damn it! Damn it!"

Dixie Mae rushed through the front door, put her slender hands on Buster's arms and laid her head on his muscular back. "Buster," she said in a soft voice like a bluebird singing in the early morning. "It can't be anything too big for us to work out together." She released her hold on him and sat in the swing slowly. "I don't know, but I feel it in my bones, and I prayed about it. The answer is right here in our midst. We have to look real hard, though." Dixie Mae leaned way back, closed her eyes and began to hum an old gospel song: "On a hill far away stood an old rugged cross…"

Buster looked at her sideways and shook his head. Dixie Mae could sing a song in the middle of World War Three and escape from the turmoil.

Whap! A folded newspaper hit Buster on the head. He didn't see it coming, engrossed in his dilemma, his head down digging a little hole in the red dirt. He looked quickly up and there was

Rose standing next to him. "What's going on down here?" She said between belly-rolling laughter. "Y'all ain't got nothing to do but dig up this hard-ass dirt and sleep on the porch? I came to get me some of those good ol' Georgia greens. I can smell them all the way to the house."

Dixie Mae moved over in the swing. "Come on, sit down. Dinner gone be ready soon and I got some peach pies in the stove too. How's Angela doing? Last week she was so upset. Did you get her to tell you what happened?"

Rose said, "She gonna be all right, soon as she acts like she got some sense. She always been so trusting of people. Especially men. Some attorney named Carl somebody. Now all of a sudden she fell in love. I can't understand her. He hurt her so bad she didn't want to see her own child. Now he's coming to visit her and she down there floating like a butterfly, getting all prettied up, so I just got the hell out of there. The way I feel about it, I would probably say the wrong thing and slap the shit out of him."

Buster stood up and brushed off his hands. "Well, Rose, you not going to meet him, but I think it's time somebody did."

Dixie Mae stood close to her husband. "Buster, you can't get in her business. She knows what she wants."

"Maybe she do know what she wants, but it's time Mr. Attorney Man met Old Buster!"

Rose gave Dixie Mae a surprised look and Dixie Mae gave Rose a "you can't stop him" look.

Buster left the ladies to their gossip and strode down the lane with a quiet, determined expression on his face. He thought of what he had promised his late mother—to look after all the children on this lane. And Angela was just as much one of his as all the rest. And if she wasn't, she was certainly God's child.

Buster stopped Carl at the gate before he could enter the walkway down to Angela's.

"I guess I'm sort of getting into your business, Carl," Buster said leaning on the picket fence. "But I've been through so much with that little lady and I don't want to see her hurt anymore."

"Okay," Carl sighed, "I respect that Buster. I do care for Angela quite a bit because she makes me feel good about myself. Maybe I couldn't cope with the color difference plus I went through some very hard times with my ex-wife. I still think about how she hurt me. I know Angela doesn't think she would, but she could destroy me if she chooses to and even if she doesn't."

"It seems like to me, Mr. Attorney Man," Buster looked him into the sea-green eyes, "you should leave stuff alone if you can't handle it."

Buster and Carl stood without speaking, watching cars go slowly up and down the bumpy road. The evening sun began to set, casting a bright orange glow on Park Lane. After a few minutes Carl spoke, "Well, I guess I have to try a little harder for my little Cookie." He continued in answer to Buster's puzzled look, "Angela reminds me of an old cook that my grandfather had. Seems like no one cared about him but her, because he was so onerous. Cookie always had a big smile for everyone."

Buster just stared at him.

"Yes, Sarah something or other. I can't recall the surname." Carl rubbed his thick beard. "Could have been Jenkins. I do think it was. Yes, Sarah B. Jenkins it was." He smiled, nodding his head slowly.

Buster let out a loud whoop and picked Carl right up off the ground. "Hallelujah! Hallelujah! Hallelujah!" Then he took Carl's arm and practically dragged him down the lane to his house. "Dixie Mae! Dixie Mae!" His whole face lit up. "Look! Look!"

Dixie Mae came to the door wiping her hands on her blue apron. "Buster, what you doing pulling a white man down the street in Georgia?"

Buster let go of Carl's hand, "I'm sorry, sir. You all right?"

Before Carl could answer, Buster said to Dixie Mae, "This here is old man Finch's grandson. He knew my mama."

Dixie Mae extended her hand. "Please to meet you, Mr. Finch. Sit down while I get us some coffee, and I better call Angela and tell her you down here, Carl."

Buster grinned, "Carl Finch. Right here on Park Lane. Right here in our midst. Mr. Finch, who owns this property? From the corner there at Oak Street down to the end on Stewart Lane."

Carl pondered a moment. "Buster, as far as I can recall, my grandfather left all of his worldly goods to my father, McKenzie Finch the Second, his sole heir. I never knew this lane had been included in the estate. When my grandfather passed on fifteen years ago, everything went to probate. A real mess it became. You probably know more about it than I do."

"Mr. Finch," Buster sighed, "the management company leases these duplexes to the folks here. Far as I been able to find out, the landlord is unknown or nobody would say who it is. My mother told me she had some of this land given to her."

Carl sipped his hot, sugary coffee. "Then the landlord has to be my father. Always got what he wanted. Onerous as my grandfather, he was. Left town after the settlement. Went back East somewhere. It will probably take a small miracle to locate him." He turned to Dixie Mae, "Anybody here believe in 'em?"

Chapter 7

"You can't run from God!" the short preacher shouted into the brisk night air to the growing crowd of sinners on the corner of Fifth and Lennox, on Chicago's south side. The few musicians in his mobile congregation sang out "Amen," and shook and banged the tambourines every time he paused for breath. "We need to stop running from God!" the speaker continued and pranced around the makeshift pulpit. "God's got answers for us but we are afraid to go get 'em. Some of us like to worry, be despondent, confused, depressed! Don't want nothing to go right. Singing the blues when we ought to be praising the Lord." He pointed to a few quiet members of the audience, "You been running! You been running!"

Pearce started to back away slowly from his spot at the end of the crowd. Curiosity had drawn him here, but he didn't want to be pointed out by nobody! The preacher continued calling souls and then, suddenly, he pointed to Pearce, "Stop!"

Pearce froze, and he heard his own heart beating faster and faster. He didn't know whether he should run or follow the rest of the lost souls to the altar. All eyes were on him now but he didn't move. His mind went back to when he'd been ten years old. His mother had dressed him in a blue and white three-piece suit. All eyes in the crowded Baptist church were on him then. He'd stepped forward to give his Easter speech. His mother was crying before he even started reciting the twenty-third Psalm.

Now in Chicago, with all these strangers watching him, Pearce could still picture his mother with tears rolling down her weary face. He stepped forward in a trance. But it wasn't the

crowd here on Lennox and Fifth Street coaxing him or this boisterous servant of God. He heard his mother whispering, "Go on.
Go on." Pearce sank down on the red-carpeted altar and warm,
salty tears fell from his face for the first time in all his adult
years.

The preacher spoke softly just above a whisper. "Praise the
Lord. Another soul has come to God for his salvation."

Pearce looked up as a well-dressed, feeble old white man
knelt down next to him. He had a gray chestnut beard with a
matching mustache. His bushy eyebrows wrinkled, his eyes
closed tightly.

Then the man opened his sea-green eyes and Pearce heard
him say, "I'm an alcoholic. I've been away from home too long."

The preacher comforted the stranger, "Say no more, my
brother. God knows the situation and if you truly believe in him,
he will show you the way back."

The congregation sang out, "Amen! Amen! Amen!" The tambourines shook. A woman shouted from the crowd, "Yes! Yes, he
will!"

The preacher sat down on the wooden stool, wiped perspi-
ration from his forehead and his neck and stomped his feet
several times. He stopped, bowed his head for a moment, then
he shouted, "Yes, we need to stop running."

Chapter 8

*B*uster sat with Red Jake under the weeping willow tree at Nash's fishing pond enjoying the peace and quiet on this Easter Sunday morning. Since he chose not to attend church services at Mt. Zion Temple, the next thing he could do to please Dixie Mae was to have some fresh, juicy catfish for the evening get-together. Everybody would be coming over to eat some of Dixie Mae's good cooking.

The holiday would not be the same without them feeding the whole lane. Plus, this special day gave him a reason to visit his favorite fishing place. And Buster could always depend on his companion, Red Jake, for a bottle of that special Night Train wine and some catching up on the neighborhood bullshit.

"Buster," Red Jake said, putting ice into his metal wine can. "You know how long we had these old cans?" He held his up to the sunlight, squinting his eyes at the bottom.

"Yeah, since 1939. The date is still on mine. I think we got them that first Easter morning we told our folks we'd catch the fish for supper."

Jake laughed, "What the hell were we thinking about when we wrote the date on the bottom of these old cans?"

"Well, we said one day we would be old and beat-up just like these old cans and we would still be best friends," Buster answered.

Red Jake let out a long sigh. "How you think we gon' find this McKenzie Finch the Second?"

"I don't know for sure, but his son Carl would like to find him too. Like my mama always said, 'What goes around comes around, and wherever there's something good a person will come back to it.' Let's just hope McKenzie left some good here."

Buster stood and grabbed his fishing line. "Look out, I got a big one!" He reeled the fish in, "Come on, pretty baby, come on to daddy." Buster removed the five-pound wiggling fish from the hook and threw it into Red Jake's half-full bucket, "Happy Easter, motherfucker!"

Red Jake stopped laughing and said, "Wait, wait, wait a minute." He stretched his hand over the dark green five-gallon bucket. "A word of prayer. In the name of the Father, the Son and the Holy Ghost, henceforth, now and forevermore, you are now baptized!" He picked up his wine can and poured the remaining ounce of red wine over the squirming fish.

Back on Park Lane, McKenzie Finch the Second hobbled on a silver walking cane up to the gate of Buster's yard. He slowly reached his long, wrinkled hand to lift the latch, but hesitated when a voice rang out from the sidewalk.

He turned his gray chestnut head to face a young lady with a six-inch, curly afro. She walked up holding a little boy's hand. "Ain't nobody home yet. Miss Dixie Mae's still at church and I know Buster went fishing. Miss Dixie Mae should be back in an hour when morning service is over. I'll tell 'em you came by unless you want to wait for 'em."

McKenzie Finch the Second spoke with a clean, mid-eastern accent, "I'm looking for a Miss Sarah Jenkins. You know of her?"

"No sir, but I know Buster and Miss Dixie Mae real well."

McKenzie repeated the name slowly, "Buster and Miss Dixie Mae. Are they good people?"

"Yes sir, they sure are. They bought my little Sam here these clothes for Easter 'cause Buster always wants the kids to have something nice for holidays." She proudly glanced down at her little one, dressed in a red and white jacket and navy blue shorts. "And they fixing supper for everybody 'round here. They good Christian people and Miss Dixie Mae can really sing. I bet if you go 'round the corner to the church right now you can hear her. Are you lonely, sir?" She went on without letting him answer, "Why don't you come back for supper? Miss Dixie Mae and Buster feed everybody. They don't care what you look like or where you from."

McKenzie's chestnut eyebrows came together and his sea-green eyes sparkled as a chuckle captured his pink, pasty face. "They sound like good people all right." He smiled and extended his trembling hand. "It's been a pleasure talking to you, but I didn't get your name, ma'am."

"Oops," she laughed, putting her hand over her mouth. "I'm Kartina."

He responded, "Just call me Mack. That will do just fine, and I will be on my way for the lady I'm looking for is not here." He turned and hobbled back to his ivory-colored town car.

Angela pulled a pink and white ruffled lace dress over Candi's head. "My little girl looked so pretty this morning in Sunday school. It's too bad your grandmother went on back to Los Angeles. We have to call her and tell her how pretty you looked in the dress she sent you." She gave her a big kiss on her round cheek and proceeded to dress her in a pink and white short set, and led her to the kitchen to make a milkshake. "Let me do it, Mommie." Candi climbed onto the dining chair. Angela put bananas, strawberry ice cream and milk on the table. Candi got down, went to the cabinet and struggled with a large jar of peanut butter.

"What else can we put in it?" Angela smiled and took the peanut butter. "Oh, yes, we need some ice." She threw in three cubes. "A plum? How about a juicy peach?"

"Yes, Mommie, a peach for Daddy."

Angela sat down and started to peel the banana, "Honey, Daddy won't be here to have any this time."

"Why, Mommie?"

"Daddy's tired and went away for a while to rest." Her hands shook like they did every time Candi mentioned Pearce. "Here, baby, put the banana in," Angela said softly.

Candi squashed the banana in her little fist before releasing it into the blender. She looked at Angela with a stern face. "Daddy's coming home to sleep in his bed. He's coming home now!" She began to cry.

Angela held her close, "It's okay, honey. It's okay."

"Mommie, look!" Candi pointed to the open window. Angela turned and they saw a big bouquet of yellow and orange roses. They ran and looked out but didn't see anyone or the roses. Angela's heart fluttered in excitement. They opened the back door and looked around. Still no one in sight. "I know," Angela said, "Let's just sit right here on the step and wait."

Suddenly, a muffled voice came from the side of the duplex. "Oh no, give up so soon?" It was Carl! He jumped in front of them with the flowers, "Roses for my little ladies."

Angela gave him a big hug while Candi grabbed his right leg and squeezed it as hard as she could. Angela took the roses and Carl picked up Candi, tossing her into the air. She beamed with laughter and on the way down wiped peanut butter and banana on his thick beard. He wiped his face with his hands and licked his fingers, "Ummn, good. What's that on your hands," he asked Candi as he leaned down and held her hand. "Yummie, yummie. I think I'll have some more." He opened his mouth as if to bite her hand. He laughed and turned to Angela, "You think I can get this stuff off my face in time for Buster and Dixie Mae's dinner? I decided to go after all. I just figured it might do me some good since it's Easter." He tapped Angela gently on the nose.

Candi left the table and the unfinished milkshake, "Here,

Daddy, want a peach?"

Angela returned Carl's puzzled expression with a smile and an "I don't know" look.

Buster set the sizzling roast beef on the buffet next to the corn on the cob dripping with melted butter. Then he helped Dixie Mae set the table while the first batch of catfish cooked to a golden brown in the deep fryer. Dixie Mae hummed her favorite song, "The Old Rugged Cross." The rest of the menu consisted of black-eyed peas, green beans fresh from the garden, potato salad, candied yams, turnip greens, acorn squash, pineapple and honey glazed ham, blueberry and peach cobblers, corn bread, strawberry cheesecakes, pastel-colored cupcakes and banana pudding. Buster cracked a chunk of ice over the Coca Colas and the orange and grape sodas. Eight guests were expected for the sit-down dinner. The peach-colored tablecloth had nine place settings.

"Who is the extra plate for, Dixie Mae?" Angela asked while arranging the red and yellow roses in the centerpiece.

Buster answered for Dixie Mae, "She always sets an extra plate on the table at Easter and Christmastime."

"Yes, just in case somebody drops by hungry," Dixie Mae said.

Buster joked, "Yeah, since this is Easter, Jesus Christ just might drop by."

Red Jake joined in the fun. "By the looks of all this food, he must be bringing his disciples."

Dixie Mae slapped them both on their heads with her blue dishtowel. "Y'all hurry up with the rest of that fish and don't let it burn!"

Everybody finally sat with heads bowed, holding hands and

giving thanks to God. Suddenly, a light tap-tap announced a guest at the unlatched screen door.

"Come on in," Buster called out.

All eyes turned to the door. The bottom end of a silver walking cane appeared on the burgundy throw rug. A feeble old man hobbled into the doorway, turned and faced the diners.

Carl stood up from the table and gazed at the stranger. He said very softly just above a whisper, "Father, Father, my father." Carl held him close and when he finally let go, he continued, "I can't believe I'm looking at you, and for God's sake, Father, what are you doing here right now?"

McKenzie said, "I have some business to take care of, but I must say I'm surprised to see you here myself. You're a little bit out of range yourself. Aren't you now, son?"

Everybody in the room was silent for what seemed like eternity.

"Oh, everyone, please excuse us, this is my father. I have not seen him in a while." Then he introduced him to everybody, including little Candi, who busied herself digging into the candied yam. She flashed the old man her crooked smile, "Hi Father."

Dixie Mae stood up. "Come on, please sit down. We got a plate already here for you." She took his hand and helped Carl seat him.

Dixie Mae continued, "We are going to have our Easter supper, then we gon' see what Mr. Finch is doing here in Valdosta." Her pencil-thin eyebrows came together as she gave everybody a stern look.

Buster did his best to enjoy the meal, but deep down inside he wanted to grab Mr. McKenzie Finch by the collar and ask him, "Do you know where the papers are for this land?" But he remained silent, knowing Dixie Mae would be furious if this special meal became a shambles.

In a few moments a harder tap-tap came to the screen door.

Everybody turned again. Buster said under his breath, "Must be the disciples."

"Come on in," Dixie Mae called out, giving Buster a "behave yourself" look.

This time Candi shouted, "Daddy. Daddy!" She ran to Pearce's arms. Angela sat still with a look of disbelief on her face.

Buster could not contain himself any longer. "Oh, Lord! Jesus Christ and the Devil himself at the same supper!"

Angela looked quickly at Carl's face as he turned pale. He remained silent, avoiding her glance.

Pearce said, "Excuse me, I didn't know you were having supper. How's everybody doing? I just wanted to see my wife and daughter." He flashed them his infectious smile.

Angela stood up, looked at Carl and then at Dixie Mae, "I'm sorry, I have to go." She hurried past Pearce and out of the door, just escaping his hand when he reached for her.

Pearce said to the rest of the diners, "Don't nobody worry, I'll make sure she's all right." He carried Candi out of the door with him.

Chapter 9

*A*ngela marched up the busy lane with tears in her eyes. She could hear Pearce calling her and Candi's little voice saying. "Mommie, wait!"

Angela went inside the house and all the way through to the back porch. She went out and sat on the top step, shaking and furious.

Pearce stood in the doorway holding Candi in his arms. "Angela, I know I been wrong, but aren't you glad to see me just a little bit?"

Angela turned her angry face away willing him to disappear.

Pearce said, "I'm taking Candi inside for a while to play in her crib and don't go nowhere. I'll be right back. At least somebody's glad to see me."

He came back and tried to put his arms around Angela, but she pulled away, still silent and fuming. "Come on, baby, please talk to me. Say something. Give me a chance to explain."

She moved over close to the fence. Silent. Pearce turned to go back inside, "Be like that, damn it!"

Angela swung around, picked up two of Candi's wooden blocks, and threw them hard, just missing his curly head. "Why didn't you stay where you were?" she shouted at him. "We don't need you now."

"I left 'cause too many things started getting to me. I couldn't take it anymore." He walked towards her and she backed away. "What happened to 'We could work things out together'? You didn't even care how me and Candi were going to live. Well, I can't take it anymore."

She sat on the step, feeling miserable. Pearce sat beside her and she let him hold her close, too exhausted to move from him. He kissed her teary eyes, her face and her neck. His lips went down to her chest and her firm breast. "Oh, God, why did you leave me?" she moaned.

Pearce took her hand in his, "One thing I learned about you. You're stronger than me. You do better under pressure, and I knew so many people loved you and Candi. I knew you would make it, even better than me. I had to be by myself for a while." He continued kissing her face, her chest and her firm breast.

Angela felt better now, stood with him and let him lead her inside to the bed, where he undressed her while his lips kept covering her slender body. A familiar longing crept through her. She placed her fingers in his hair, and temporarily shut out the world.

Suddenly, Carl's face appeared in her mind. She stiffened now, remembering the hurt look he had when Pearce walked in at Buster's. And Angela had told Carl that she would never hurt him.

She rolled over and got out of the bed, wrapped her blue robe around her, and sat in the side chair.

Pearce sat up and lit a cigarette. "Okay, who you been sleeping with? That man who gave you those roses in the kitchen? Who's Carl?"

"Just somebody wanted to be my friend." Angela knew better than to tell Pearce she had made love to Carl, for her sake as well as Carl's right now.

Pearce put his cigarette out in the ashtray and continued, "Are you sleeping with him?"

She lied, "No, he became a friend to me when I needed one. He treated me good. He cared about me and Candi. I didn't know what you were going to do. Maybe I'm not as strong as you thought."

"You don't need him anymore. I'm giving myself up to the police in Los Angeles, but I need to know if you are still with me. I can't keep running away. Nothing means more to me now than you and Candi."

Pearce went on explaining how much he missed her and wanted to make things work this time. But her thoughts drifted to Carl. She wondered what he must be thinking about her. She didn't know what to do with Pearce saying he needed her and Carl having been so good to her. What could she say to either man?

Pearce said, "Who was that old man at Buster's house at the table? He looks like somebody I seen before."

"Somebody Buster knows. Where do you think you saw him?"

"Somewhere in Chicago. One night at a church service."

Angela looked at him with new interest. "You went to church?"

Pearce answered, "Yeah, but then it was outside and it was getting dark and, oh well, it could have been anybody. That's why I came back. I know God wants me to stop running."

Angela became angry again. "You don't know how many nights I laid awake crying and pleading with God to let me hear just one word from you. Just one word, one word to let me know you were okay." She walked around the small bedroom with her arms up in despair. "I begged and pleaded with you through all the ups and downs. Through all your hurt and confusion, but I loved you and I thought we had something worth fighting for, worth holding on to."

Pearce lay back on the bed without saying a word. Angela walked over to the crib where Candi lay sleeping with her thumb in her mouth. "Look at that baby! So many nights we held each other and cried ourselves to sleep wishing for you." Her voice softened after she sat back in the chair, "Now you tell me that God wants you to stop running."

Pearce sat up on the side of the bed looking sincere, "I'll make it up to you."

"There's only one thing you can do now. Go back to L.A. right now. Show me right now." Angela stared into his honey eyes. He stared into her ebony eyes. Nobody moved.

After a few minutes, Angela walked away from him and went into the living room. She sat in the big chair with her legs crossed Indian style and held her head down in her hands.

Pearce threw on his shirt and shorts. "I'll be back and we can talk more about this."

Angela said nothing, still sitting. Pearce walked to the front door, turned around and said, "You have to stay with me, baby." He took a deep breath and went on out the door.

Pearce walked past Red Jake's Pool Hall to the back door of Danielle's apartment. He sighed and knocked with his usual tap, tap, tap. Danielle opened the door with surprise on her meticulously made-up face. The sun-streaked red hair lay on her narrow shoulders just like Pearce remembered.

She threw her velvet-smooth arms around him. "Pearce, where you been? I worried so much about you. I thought you was dead." She put her hand inside his shirt, rubbed his hairy chest and started to kiss his face. "I missed you. I missed you." He stiffened under her touch. She stepped back and looked at him.

"Danielle, I need to talk to you, seriously. I know I owe you an explanation. Why I left."

"I don't care why you left right now. I just need to hold you, touch you." She reached out and put her fingers in his hair and tried to kiss his face.

"No, for real. I'm serious." He sat on her blue and white crushed velvet sofa. Silver moonlight shone through the white satin curtains. The only other light in the apartment came from the tiny antique lamp in the corner of the large formal dining room. Pearce glanced out of an oval window and saw Red Jake's Pool Hall, which was closed in honor of Easter. The "Gone

Fishing" sign placed in the window.

Danielle sat next to him, her head to one side and her hands folded in her lap. "Talk to me."

"Look," he said, "I gotta straighten out my life. I know you been good to me, but Angela needs me to be good to her now. I've caused her too much pain. You told me yourself that she must have loved me a lot to come all the way to Georgia with me in all this trouble." He looked at her with anguish on his face. "I even left my daughter, Danielle." He stood and headed for the door. "I have to go now. I'm sorry. I have to stop running."

Danielle stood quietly, "That's the way you want it?" she said softly.

"Yes, that's the way I want it."

Danielle turned, facing the window with her arms folded. Silence filled the room. She turned suddenly, "Then get the hell out. What are you waiting for? Get out!" She opened the closet and started throwing his clothes at him. "Go on! That's the way you want it."

He watched her, his eyes wide with shock. He thought she wanted him to be good to Angela. When she started throwing her beveled mirror and hairbrush at him, he hurried through the door just missing one of her red heels upside his head. She ran outside after him, "And don't come crawling back to me when you can't take it no more!"

Pearce walked down the dark street with his few items of clothing in a bundle. He turned the corner thinking how good it would be now that he freed himself from one obstacle in his life. He resolved to be courageous and straighten out the rest of his life. He was still a young man. Just twenty-seven. Running away to Chicago to make things better. Nothing but strangers there. Now he had his family to keep together.

He spotted a trash bin in an alley along his route. Yes, get rid of old baggage. He reached over and tossed the bundle away and saw three green and white police cars with the lights flashing. Habit and instinct made him duck back around the corner out of sight. Pearce stood in that spot, his heart thumping. Suddenly he heard one of the officers say, "We got him. Over here!" Pearce squatted low behind the trash bin and watched three white officers force a dark-skinned boy, about fourteen years old, to put his hands up and lean on the squad car. The orange lights kept flashing and lit up most of the run down dark alleyway.

Pearce heard the boy say, "I didn't do nothing. I was just going around the corner to see my sister."

One officer pointed his revolver at him while another one searched his pockets, taking a few bills and some change out.

"Oh yeah?" the first officer challenged the boy. "If you didn't rob that store, what you doing walking around with all this money? Look at all this money." He let it fall to the ground and turned to the next officer, "Don't that look like cash to you?"

"Yeah," the second officer answered. "Too much cash for a kid with holes in his shoes."

The first officer said surprised, "Holes in his shoes. Where?"

The second officer answered, "Right there." He poked the boy's left foot hard with his nightstick. Then he stuck his right foot hard. "And a big hole there!"

The boy cried out with pain. Pearce could barely make out his muffled reply, "My mama gave me the money to take to my sister. She need it to buy milk for her baby." He whimpered, "I didn't do nothing wrong. You can ask my mama."

The first officer said, "Don't put your mama in this, boy. She'd be better off without a punk like you." He put his handcuffs on the boy and pushed him into the squad car. All the cars left the scene.

Pearce tried to compose himself and all he could do then was to go slowly back to Danielle's place. He tapped on the door three times. She opened it wearing a white silk teddy that clung to her caramel-colored body. She stood there leaning on the open door with her pink lips smiling.

She took his hand, led him into the bedroom and laid down with him on her heart-shaped waterbed. The black-and-white tiger bedspread felt cool under his skin. Neither spoke a word. Danielle unbuttoned his shirt, kissed his chest and made circles around his nipples with her soft tongue.

"I couldn't make it, Danielle," he said as she removed his slacks.

"Shhh…don't talk, baby. Forget about it now." She massaged his tired legs and thighs, then turned him over, rubbed his shoulders and back, kissed his neck and nibbled his ears. Soon he relaxed and all thought went out of his mind except her lilac perfume and her hard nipples under her silk teddy.

Chapter 10

Angela remained in her position in the chair until she heard Carl outside the front door. She ran out and went straight into his arms where she felt good, safe for a while. "Carl, I didn't know he'd be coming back today. Okay, yes, I expected him to return someday, and I told you he could show up at any time."

Carl held her face in his hands and looked into her eyes, "What about us?"

Angela turned her head away and took a deep breath. Turning back to him, she said, "I don't know what to do now. I just don't know."

Carl went on, "I know I hurt you when I didn't show up at the airport. But I came right back 'cause I knew I had no real reason to hurt you. Is that what you are afraid of? That I may disappoint you again?"

"Maybe."

Carl held her by the shoulders, trying with tenderness to keep her attention on him. "Your eyes are sad and dull now. No matter what I may do, Cookie, I'll always come back to you."

"I need time. I just can't give you answers now."

"You're not going to let him back into our life after he deserted you? Look at me and tell me you're not doing that, Angela."

"You don't understand the things I have to do. God knows I want to tell you but I just can't. I think he needs me."

This time Carl held Angela tighter by the shoulders, "He needs you, but I want you. What do you want?" He waited a moment for her to answer and when she didn't he released his hold and started to back away. She took his hand and squeezed it. "Can you wait a while?"

He walked down to the sidewalk, stretching his arms up into the air. "I don't know. I don't know!" He turned to look at her. Angela smiled, which took a lot of effort. Carl saluted her and left.

Angela went inside the screen door, letting it hang open behind her. What could she do now? God, she wished she could talk to her mother in Los Angeles, but the F.B.I. probably still had her mother's phone tapped, thinking she would call and they would find her and Pearce. Besides, Angela knew what Rose would say about Pearce. Leave that fool alone and go ahead and be happy. She knew her mother meant well, but Angela felt she had to have answers from God now. She'd think about what Carl said, what Pearce wanted, what her mother would say, what God tells her and then do what she had to. Angela sat in the chair again and prayed.

Pearce walked in and switched on the lamp. By the look on his face, she knew he would not turn himself in.

He started, "Angela…"

Angela stood. "It's okay, Pearce. Everything is all right now. I'm not angry anymore." She smiled, held his hand, guiding him to the bed where she sat, and placed his head in her lap. She smelled an unfamiliar lilac perfume, but said nothing. She kept rubbing his head until he relaxed and closed his eyes.

After he went to sleep, she stood up and walked slowly to the phone. The answer she wanted was clear now.

Carl Finch walked up the winding hill to the small cemetery one mile from Park Lane. Many of the lonesome tombstones were covered with partial Easter bouquets of white and lavender lilies. The sun had long gone, leaving him at the mercy of the scarce lighting from the distant fence posts. He reached his family's section and sat on the soft, moist grass between two plots that had been well kept by him and his brother, Steven, despite the long absence of his father, McKenzie Finch the Second.

Carl, shook up by Pearce's sudden appearance, had left Dixie Mae's dinner after a brief reuniting with his father, whom he left in the care of Buster and Red Jake. Let them fight about the property because right now he had a broken heart to put back together.

He looked down at his mother's, Jessica Finch's, headstone. Then he turned to his grandfather's grave on the other side of him.

All is quiet here except for an occasional firefly chirping along with boisterous crickets. Carl began speaking to these deceased kinfolk as he did at times when he felt distressed, "Mother, you said you would always be with me, so you must know what I am going through, but just in case you don't know, I need help. You know how hurt I was before I met Angela. She made my heart sing. And just when I started to love her, her husband came back and I know he wants her, too."

Carl turned to the other grave. "Grandfather, you know Mother always sent me to you if she didn't have the answer. You two I could depend on. Father drank most of the time and couldn't do much to help himself. He showed up today, too. Says he wants to do good. His favorite phrase. Maybe this time he can."

He stopped talking while he kneeled on the wet grass and wiped the dirt off the letters on the marble headstones with his white handkerchief. He continued, "Please show me what to do about Angela. I'm afraid to hold onto her, yet, I'm afraid to let go." He threw his hands up into the darkness. "What the hell can I do? I love her!"

Suddenly, he heard an old voice, "Your grandfather never gave up a fight! He didn't quit when things got rough. He wouldn't give in to a chicken!"

Carl looked around, blinking his eyes. The voice continued, "Not even a drunken one!"

Carl found his voice, "Father…"

There stood Buster and Red Jake holding on to McKenzie Finch the Second, leading him to this spot in the cemetery.

Carl asked, "What are you three doing up here?"

Buster and Jake stood there with anxious looks on their faces. Then Buster scratched his head with an odd twist on his lips, "Your father just told us something."

Carl stared at his father, who sat with the help of Buster and Red Jake.

McKenzie began, "Son, I know I've been away from you for a long time, and I never did much by you and your brother. Your mother died at such a young age, I couldn't see life as being fair anymore. Something happened to me. Blame it on alcohol. I don't have all the answers. But I knew that this man's mother," he pointed to Buster, "Sarah Jenkins, is the rightful owner of the property from Park Lane to Ruby Street. I knew it when my father, your grandfather, lay dying. He placed the document in my care. He wrote it on his deathbed in the presence of Miss Sarah."

Carl showed deep concern now. "What happened, Father?"

"Well, at the time she was on in age herself. Sickly too. I didn't think she could handle it. I told her I would see that everything be done properly. I kept the document until after Father's funeral. Then buried it with him." Tears fell down McKenzie's red cheeks. "I placed the property into the hands of the management company and left the state. I figured no one would believe an old, ailing colored woman. I had intentions of coming back to make things right, but after so much time passed, I didn't know the way to do it."

After a long pause, Carl said, "I can't believe this! Didn't grandfather leave you, yourself, very heavily endowed?" He stood up, prancing around in his famous courtroom manner, throwing questions at his father. "And you say you knew this woman personally. And did she not assist you many a night when you became inebriated? Did she not make excuses to your father for you to save your hide?"

Buster and Jake sat down, remained silent and stared at the tombstone of McKenzie Finch Senior.

McKenzie the Second answered, "Your grandfather thought me to be irresponsible. I kept the land because I didn't understand at the time how much it meant to him for her to have it. I thought he did it to spite me."

Carl continued, "But you say you were there when he wrote the document in question. Surely you must have known. Isn't it a fact that you wanted everything for yourself and had no regard for a man who left you, yourself, so well endowed? A man near death? Isn't it a fact that you robbed a poor black woman of what she gave of herself so unselfishly for?"

"I came back to Valdosta because I know now what goodness means." McKenzie looked at Buster, Red Jake and back again at his son. He stood up slowly, leaning on his silver cane, looking up at Carl, straight into his eyes, sticking his wrinkled finger in his face almost touching his freckled nose. "Yes, Mr. Attorney, I came back. Goddamn it!"

Buster spoke, "Well, move over Carl Finch, we got work to do. We gon' dig up some dry bones!"

Red Jake widened his eyes. "Wait a minute, wait a minute, wait a minute! I done been through a lot of crazy things with you, Buster, but ain't no way you gon' git me to dig up somebody's grave. And how we know he ain't just telling a tale?"

All eyes then turned to McKenzie, who said, "Because there's something gold in there."

Red Jake eyed Buster. Buster eyed Red Jake. Jake took the shovel out of Buster's hands. "I'll start digging while you get the backhoe from the truck."

Carl jumped up, "You're not going to dig up Grandfather's grave! You need a court order. This is entirely against the laws of Georgia!"

Buster held out a long pitchfork. "Start digging, Mr. Attorney Man. You got a stake in this too."

"Oh yeah, do I?"

"Your old man here could be your next defendant. I do believe stealing is also entirely against the laws of Georgia. Or is it, Mr. Attorney Man? And what would your kind, old grandfather think about it?"

Carl opened his mouth to speak, and Buster held out his hand. "Wait. Sometimes you have to take matters into your own hands." Red Jake stood closer to Buster's side and leaned on the shovel, and Buster continued, "Plus, I think you outnumbered. Even your father is on our side. You can help or you can watch, but this here grave of McKenzie Finch Senior is gon' be dug up tonight! Jake, go get some rope from the truck so we can help Mr. Attorney Man sit still."

Carl threw up his hands and said, "Okay, okay. I can't stop you but I won't help you either." He folded his arms across his chest and turned his chestnut head away.

Buster operated the backhoe while Jake worked with the shovel.

Carl said, "You must realize that the caretaker could send the sheriff if they see something suspicious going on."

Night owls hooted back and forth to one another throughout the laborious digging. The dark sky turned a deeper shade of black during one of the longest hours of Buster's life. Carl and

McKenzie sat quietly until Buster moved enough hard dirt to reach the wooden box. Carl turned his head away. McKenzie turned his head. Red Jake laid down his shovel and turned his head.

Buster said a prayer, and gathered the courage to lift the lid. He heard his own breathing in the quiet night and felt his heart pounding in his chest. The owls hooted, and the rusted hinges squeaked when he took a deep breath and opened the top quickly.

Buster gasped at the contents and his stomach churned from the dry musty odor. Long gray hair. Dry bones. A dark blue double-breasted suit. A red hankie. Dust everywhere. Buster couldn't move.

McKenzie spoke, "Reach behind the handkerchief, goddamn it!"

In a trance, Buster reached his gritty hand behind the handkerchief into the suit pocket and retrieved a leather pouch.

He quickly closed the box. Everybody gathered around as he took a folded paper from the pouch and helped him to read it. The document, still intact, said, "This property is left to my longtime friend and cook, Mrs. Sarah B. Jenkins." It was signed and dated July 1, 1957. Witnessed by McKenzie Finch the Second. The signature was plain and fully legible, and on the bottom of the parchment paper was another signature written in big gold letters, McKenzie Finch Senior.

Carl assured them that the document answered all the legal aspects, and Buster and Red Jake hurried to place the dark brown chunks of grass and left the old man in peace. They gathered up the equipment, satisfied with the mission accomplished, assisted McKenzie down the unsteady hill and got into Buster's old truck as fast as they could.

"I knew somebody would see us!" said Carl as they all looked around to see headlights approaching from the winding road at the bottom of the hill.

"Step on it, Buster," cried Red Jake from the rear of the pickup.

Buster cranked and cranked and cranked, but the old truck wouldn't start. "Whoever it is, I hope they got some gas," Buster said. He raised his fist up in anger, "Oh shit! Of all the damn times to run out of gas, this motherfucker does it in the fucking graveyard."

McKenzie said, "Don't worry. We're in the right place 'cause we're all dead now." The car came all the way up to them, the lights shining a white glare right into their eyes. The car stopped, turned off the lights and they saw it was Dixie Mae in Buster's big Buick. She leaned out of the car and said, "Lord, have mercy! I knew you all was up to something. What y'all doing up here disturbin' the dead?"

They all looked at her with sheepish grins on their faces and then all looked at one another.

Buster said, "I'll tell you everything later. Now the truck is out of gas and we need to leave here and put this Easter Sunday behind us." They sat silently in the car while Buster drove and Dixie Mae hummed the soft notes to "On a hill far away stood an old rugged cross."

Chapter 11

The next morning Pearce woke up and looked at the alarm clock on the table. "Wow, I didn't know I slept to ten o'clock. What you been doing all morning?" He looked at Angela and jumped out of bed. "What are you doing? What you packing for? Where you think you going?"

Angela had placed her big worn-out suitcase on the side chair and she stood next to it rapidly putting Candi's clothing in it. "I'm going back to Los Angeles tonight. The time has come for me to leave." She walked over to the closet and took out another small suitcase.

"You're leaving without giving me a chance. I just came back. I know your mother been talking to you again about going back. Why do you listen to your mother over me? She don't know what we been through." He started removing the clothes from the suitcase. "Tell her you and Candi ain't going nowhere. Your mother is always mixing in our business!"

Angela put the clothes back in the suitcase as she said, "I am leaving. If I listened to my mother I wouldn't be here with you at all. You did what you had to do when you felt like it. Now, I am leaving!"

He looked at her with threatening eyes, "What you gonna do if I don't let you go?"

"Just like you did everything to stay away from prison bars, I'll do everything I can to get out of this bondage."

"Angela, wait a minute. Sit down for just a few minutes and think about the whole situation again. Please just think about it before you finish packing."

Angela sat in the chair and Pearce left the room. She sat and thought about her brief meeting with Carl this morning at the donut shop when she had told him about her plans.

Carl stirred his coffee and played with his croissant. "I know you have to do what you think is best for you and Candi, but I'm going to miss you. I hate to see you go. Is it okay if I come see you?"

"I don't know. All I do know is it is time for me to go back home. You know how I love you and I will probably love you for a long time." She got up to leave.

Carl stood up. "Cookie, let me hold you one more time."

"If you hold me, I won't be able to go." She started crying.

"At least shake my hand again. Remember how we met?" He extended his hand.

Angela backed away, "No, no, no." She shook her head and walked towards Park Lane. She looked back one more time giving him her best smile. He raised his right hand and gave her a quick salute.

"Mommie, Mommie," Candi startled her back to reality, climbing on the bed holding her rag doll. "Can we take Tina?"

Angela looked at Pearce standing in the doorway. "Sure, baby, but we have to get all of her clothes, too." She smiled at Candi and continued packing.

That evening, Angela held Candi's little hand in hers and walked to the wooden bench, waiting for the train bound for Los Angeles.

"Where we going, Mommie?" Candi asked for the fifth time, holding her rag doll. Angela felt nervous about Pearce actually letting them go, so she just told Candi they were going somewhere. The big engine rolled down the tracks and braked at the passenger gate, sending huge clouds of blue smoke twirling through the night air.

Angela sat Candi on the narrow bench, put her little blue

and pink doll on her lap and said to her, "One day when you are real, real big," Angela stretched her arms overhead to show how big, "and walk like this," she mimicked the sideways gait of an old lady, "you will have a granddaughter. She will sit on your lap just like your doll, Tina here, and you will tell her about when you were just a tiny girl. You will say to her, 'Once upon a time, my mommie took me on the midnight train to freedom.'"

The conductor shouted, "All aboard!" The engine went clang, clang, clang. Other passengers hurried on. Angela and Candi advanced to the train, both mimicking the gait of an old lady. The conductor waited patiently while Angela stopped, picked up Candi and turned her around and around. They laughed together and boarded the train. The conductor pushed a button and the heavy door closed.

Pearce sat in his Chevy, where he had witnessed the happy scene. Still in a daze, he could not believe Angela would actually leave him. And he was certain that Danielle would not believe it either. He had followed Angela and Candi, needing to see for himself if she would really do it. Now, he started his car and went back to Park Lane.

Carl Finch continued the process of straightening out the property issue for Buster. He sat at his desk going over the blueprints for the new construction. He said to his secretary, "Praline, I'm still amazed at how sure Buster was that he'd find the document. These plans were drawn three years ago."

She answered, "Yes, it is amazing because you all just found the document three days ago. Some people just don't give up when they believe in something."

"I suppose one would say Buster is like my onerous grandfather, an old cuss who didn't let anybody get in the way of what he wanted." Carl set the plans neatly on his desk with a paperweight on top and stood up. "Well, that's all I can do with that. Now I have some major plans of my own."

"Sir?"

"Book me on a flight to Los Angeles. It's about time I did some business out there."

"Round-trip, sir?"

"Yes, I suppose I'll be coming back soon enough, but my father told me never give in to a chicken so next time out it will surely be one-way."

Excerpt

*Here's an excerpt from Abrendal Austin's next novel featuring
Angela Jones. Log on to www.blackpennypress.com for details and
publication date.*

— • —

The train stopped in San Diego at three in the morning.
Most of the passengers had been asleep, including Candi in the
seat between Angela and her new friend Viola. Viola had also
boarded the train in Valdosta, and she and Candi took a liking to
each other right away. It was as if they had known each other for
some time. Their new friend was kinda plump with a round,
shiny face, and Angela guessed her to be old enough to be her
mother. She was well-dressed and smelled like jasmine. The
conductor announced a thirty-minute delay and all who wanted
to get off and re-board could do so as long as they showed their
ticket stubs again.

Viola yawned and stretched her short legs. "I would get off
but I'm not sure I want to do any walking just yet. I can't walk
too fast since I broke my right foot. I'll mess around and miss
the train, and my grandchildren would not understand. You go
on, get some exercise. Candi be alright sleeping right here next
to me."

Angela really wanted to look around just a little and she
hated sitting still too long. She got up, squeezed past Viola's
knees and leaned down to kiss Candi when Viola quietly shooed
her away. Angela slowly started up the aisle and quickly turned

around and held up both hands and mouthed, "Ten minutes." Viola nodded her head then put her hand on Candi's shoulder and leaned back with her eyes closed. Angela hurried up and left the train before she changed her mind and went into the depot. She made her way to a magazine rack and started glancing through the *Ebony* magazine article on how to dress for the city you are in. She looked down at her black-laced boots and wondered if they were out of place for the city she was going to, the city she was in now or the city she just left. Now, she thought, my leather purse might work but it is a little small. She hated big purses. They always made her look smaller than her five-foot-two frame.

There were three people in line at the counter waiting to buy tickets to Los Angeles. She kept glancing back at the train and she could see Viola nodding at her letting her know that everything was okay onboard. Angela heard feet shuffling behind her so she turned around and saw a heavyset lady dressed in a red, torn coat approaching her. Her black eyes were so small Angela wondered how she could see. Also they were bloodshot, matching her outfit.

Even with air-conditioning on, Angela detected the scent of days-old dirt and sweat. The stranger opened her ruby mouth showing brown, crooked teeth and barely uttered, "Let me, Pusha, all-knowing, tell your future for just five dollars."

Angela looked in disbelief at Pusha's velvet black turban sprinkled with tiny silver stars and certainly thought this could be a fortune-teller. She thought about Candi, "I have to get back to the train."

She put the magazine away and suddenly had had enough of San Diego. She walked towards the door, looking sideways at Pusha. "I'm sorry, I have to go now."

Pusha followed her slowly with her callused hands held out, "Just five dollars for the good of mankind." Her plea was louder now, and travelers in the depot had turned their attention to the two of them. Pusha continued, "Fight the forces of evil!"

Angela turned and hurried to the train. The woman continued, "Go on, run away from your destiny." She raised her hands in the air, raising and lowering her head shouting, "For you uncaring soul. The curse of the gods be upon you." Pusha continued waving her hands. "Curses! Curses! And all that you touch!" Her belly shook with laughter.

Angela finally found her seat, held her child and looked out of the window to see Pusha approaching someone else.

Viola laughed out loud. "Honey, I know you wanted to see San Diego, but I guess you satisfied now." The laughter ceased when Angela didn't share the humor. "Just say your prayers child 'cause you know that crazy woman has nothing to do with the God we serve. She just wanted to make a quick dollar." Viola closed her eyes and muttered, "I guess we in California."

Angela remained silent and wondered what was ahead of her and why she was always so fucking curious. She fluffed the pillow under her head and started to close her eyes when a well-dressed, young Chinese man came towards Angela and Viola's row with a large, green envelope in his right hand. He stopped, looked at Angela and courteously bowed his head. "Excuse me, Miss Jones, I bring for you important news." He handed her the envelope. "You must read before train goes."

To Be Continued...

www.abrendalaustin.com